The Chronicles of Brendonia

GLANTIS TREFMORE

AWAKENING

G. C. Schop

THE
SCHOP

Commerce, Michigan

The online website provides access to books for sale as well as various blogs written to and for readers. Keep in touch, ask questions, download free content, and discover more about the author himself.

Visit **TheSchop.com**

FOR MY ENTIRE FAMILY,
FOR MY TEACHERS AND STUDENTS,
AND EVERYONE WHO BELIEVED IN ME.

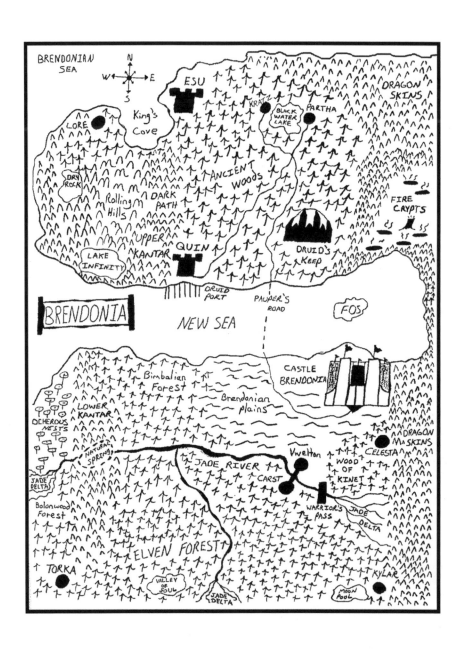

CONTENTS

PROLOGUE

THE GIFT

O N THE WESTERN SIDE OF BRENDONIA rests Lake Infinity with its clear waters rippling in the cool wind. It was late evening and the skies were unusually dark. Silence whispered over the continent, a howling wind seemingly foretelling of something evil. Yet, all seemed normal, the moon and stars beginning to sparkle among the skies as the last piece of the sun vanished behind the horizon.

The wind began to pick up, creating a whistling as the gusts blew through the deep valleys of the Rolling Hills. Streaks of moonlight shined on the hilltops, leaving the valleys in shadow. Without warning, black shadows began to climb the hills, forming black dots on the lighted hilltops.

The dark shadows disappeared as they dipped down into the valley and reappeared when reaching the top of another hill. The shadows glided silently over the hills never wavering in direction. They moved southwest toward Lake Infinity, but these were not shadows. They were figures of the night, druids, people from the twin towns of Partha and Kratz. They were a cult of humans that had twisted and turned their ways into things of greed and evil, a culture that closed themselves off from all the other races in Brendonia. Long ago, they tried to rebel against Brendonian rule, yet the armies of Castle Brendonia drove them back to their territory in the Ancient Woods. Sheer size and force fended off the druids. Their greed for land and rule had unnecessarily cost them many lives, cutting their numbers by half. Even then, a handful of druids could perform strange magic that killed many Brendonians.

An unfamiliar sound echoed from the trees surrounding Lake Infinity. A man cloaked in black robes stepped out from behind a tree. The man was very tall and stocky. His hood was back, and the moonlight shined on his flawless face. An impressive-looking black beard covered his chin, neutralized by two innocent blue eyes; eyes that almost glowed. He watched the shadowy figures approaching in the distance.

The man began to speak softly to himself, "So it is true. What the immortal gods have told me is true. The one of evil is already in existence, a druid with magical powers that can draw life from things and break them apart. The destruction of the lands is also true and the evil rulers will eventually take over all of Brendonia. The gods laugh at this. 'Fun and games' they call it. 'Worry not, Pantos,' they say to me. 'In time, good will conquer evil, and the races and lands will replenish.'"

Pantos turned again to the Rolling Hills. He watched six cloaked figures walk down a nearby hill. They were now only minutes away from Lake Infinity. Pantos looked upon them coldly from his hidden position. A tear began to form in his eye.

"Forgive me, immortals of the sky. I am one of your kind and of your godly blood, but I can see no game in death of innocent mortals. I cannot see the reasons behind letting this evil spread across the lands." Pantos began to tighten his bodily muscles, trying to adjust to his human form. "I may not be able to stop these evils myself. Being immortal, my stronger powers are ineffective on the mortal plane of existence, but I can help in an inadvertent way. 'Interference' as you call it, gods, the worst crime an immortal can perform. This I must do. Whatever the punishment, I will serve it, but not without reason." Pantos turned, seeing the druids nearing the lakeshore. The immortal walked behind a tree and disappeared in a dim flicker of white light.

The six druids gathered around the shores of Lake Infinity. Five vates, meaning *followers of the dark one,* wore forest-green robes and stood silent behind their leader. The master druid stood in silence, caressing the rippling waters with his eyes.

This was Bernac, the strongest in the arts of dark, druid magic. He wore black robes and remained hooded, concealing his facial features. The dark figure began to speak in a hiss. "I trust all my plans are understood and will be followed as soon as our task is finished?"

The five vates nodded, uttering no words.

"Remember," Bernac raised his voice. "After I conjure this strong magic, it will take me 15 years to regain my strength through an undisturbed sleep. When I awake, the druid population should be fully restored and powerful enough to claim all of Brendonia for ourselves. I give you this warning. Follow all my plans accordingly, but do not execute any attack until I awake." Bernac finished his words and waved the five vates to surround the northern half of the lake. The druid highmaster waited until they were in position, then with a half-smile concealed beneath his hood, whispered to himself, "Ready yourselves people of Brendonia. Fifteen years from this night the druids will rise to power once again, only this time with a force 1,000 times greater than before." With this, Bernac stepped onto Lake Infinity's waters. The highmaster druid walked on the water as if it were a moist forest floor. He seemingly glided to the center of the lake where he commenced to raise his hands. Bernac mumbled unknown words as his body descended into the lake, vanishing beneath its clear, fresh water.

The five green-robed vates also murmured the words of magic, supplying their lord with what power they could. The lake began to bubble as thunder rumbled in the sky. Rain began to pour down as great gusts of wind shook the trees. Black clouds masked the moon. Nowhere did its light touch the land. The five vates murmured unknown words, their minds meeting each other. Their minds became one with the dark master, Bernac. The vates held up twisted hands as ten blackish beams of light shot forth into Lake Infinity. Immediately, the lake's waters turned as black as the five vates' eyes.

Bernac stood on the lake's bottom with his hands reaching toward the vates above. A black aura of light began to form around Bernac's body. The misty cloud began to grow outward, spreading throughout the entire lake. The druid highmaster's body shuddered as his hands wrenched back, sending forth a burst of black incandescent light.

The vates instantly broke off their spell. They watched as the black light pushed forward leaving the lake clear again. The black light formed a thin line on Lake Infinity's southern shore. Quickly, the vates grasped each other's hands, forming a circle, and disappeared from the scene, leaving only a misty cloud that slowly dispersed into the night air.

Without warning, a wall of black fire shot upward into the sky. Thunder followed, shaking the ground as the black mass of fire spread in a thread-like line across the entire continent. As the line reached the Eastland, it completely turned in a half-circle and came back, only this time even further south of Lake Infinity. Then, with one earth-shattering boom, the black fire covered its magical drawing and vanished from sight, along with the entire landmass it had covered. It had devoured a complete forest and even the center of the vast Kantar Mountains, destroying every living thing within its borders. As rain poured down from the sky, massive amounts of water from the Brendonian Sea rushed into the empty hole created by the magical fire. Only the thunder could match the noise of the roaring water that flowed into the open space creating the New Sea in this great aftermath. Saltwater now replaced the beautiful forests and mountains that once covered the land.

Ashlena struggled through the forest to reach her small home in the town of Oulhaven. She had been out gathering herbs for a stew, and when reaching down to pull some roots, a small snake bit her on the wrist. Fifteen minutes had passed since then, and the poison was spreading throughout her body. She knew the best way to prevent the poison from spreading was to lie still; however, she had no choice but to keep moving. Ashlena lived alone, and no one in town knew she had left. She only planned to be gone a few hours, returning before nightfall. The townswoman was having trouble interpreting landmarks that would lead her safely back home. The pain was throbbing through her frail body, and she did not know how much longer she could continue.

Ashlena, a woman in her twenties just beginning life, who was now facing its end, blinked back tears of fright. Brushing her blond hair away from brown eyes blurred with tears, Ashlena struggled to find her way home. Her breathing was heavy, and the brittle night air was painful to her dry throat. The forest trees were spinning around her as the poison spread throughout her body, causing dizziness. With a weakened cry for help, she fell harshly to the ground. Ashlena tried to scream out again, but her voice was too weak. Swelling began to develop everywhere on her body and her throat constricted from the venom. Slowly, she slipped into unconsciousness.

Without warning, her body glowed with white light. Instantly, she was awake, as if aroused from a deep sleep. Ashlena felt ridiculous lying on the forest floor. Removing her face from the ground, she slowly picked her head up to look around. Remembering the snakebite, she quickly discovered the mark on her wrist was gone. No sign of swollen tissue remained. Ashlena laughed at herself, thinking she had fallen asleep and dreamt the whole thing. She stood up and began brushing off dirt and leaves.

She stopped moving altogether. Ashlena sensed something behind her, the presence of another person or some *thing*. As she built up enough courage, she turned around. She let out a heave of relief as she found nothing save the forest trees. Upon turning, however, a dark figure drifted through the forest toward her. Her first instinct was to run, but she found it impossible. Some force was holding her in that very spot.

"Do not be afraid. I mean you no harm," the voice gently beckoned.

A strange feeling of calmness came over her as the man lowered his hood. She did not know the stranger, but sensed she should. "What do you want of me?"

"I've come to give you a chance to live a second life," the black-robed figure said in the most serious of tones.

"I know not what you speak of, sir," Ashlena suspiciously told the stranger.

There was a long pause as small rumbles of thunder sounded to the far west. "It was not a dream, Ashlena," he said as his face became sad.

The young woman stuttered in confusion, "…but I'm fine …what?"

"I am Pantos. I am an immortal, a god from the sky. My punishment is certain now that I have changed your fate. Tonight, Ashlena, you were destined to die, but at the very moment your time came, I intervened and healed you. This world, your world, is threatened by a great evil, and the gods do not plan to stop it. Fifteen years from now, the druids from upper Brendonia are going to once again attempt to control all of Brendonia."

"What? The druids are harmless now. They haven't been a threat for years." Ashlena questioned harshly, feeling she had this fraud by his tongue. Brendonia was one land. There was no such thing as upper Brendonia.

Pantos realized it would take too long for her to comprehend his words. They were just too much to believe. The god raised his hands while uttering a strange incantation. Immediately, visions of sight and sound transferred into Ashlena's mind; each vision explained by the soft voice of Pantos. First, pictures of her homeland flowed through her mind as if they were her own memories. She saw humans like herself as well as many strange species unknown to her: little people in miniature homes, slender creatures with translucent bodies, and creatures of beauty and evil at the same time. He then showed her images that took place long before her birth such as the Boundary Wars and how the druids attempted to enslave the humans of Brendonia. She beheld visions of the druids Pantos had just seen at Lake Infinity only moments ago. Lastly, he recreated her struggle to reach her home in Oulhaven, and with that, the thoughts and visions faded.

"Understand that if the druids take over they will most definitely strive to possess and control all of Brendonia. This has already been prophesized. I, alone, am risking punishment, sacrificing myself to save the lands from this horrible destruction," Pantos finished.

"So why do you need *me*? Why did you save me from dying?" Ashlena was in a panic, disbelieving what was happening or what was going to happen. She began to realize that this man, Pantos, was truly a god. She knew nothing of these strange powers or of the mystifying visions and people he had shown her.

Pantos looked upon her with glowing blue eyes, telling her the rest with his visionary telepathy. "I need something, someone to do my bidding, someone who will have my powers and be able to stop the druids, but I'm running out of time. I ask you to undergo great physical stress. It has never been done before, and it is forbidden by the immortals, but it is the only way I can think of that might work. Will you help me create…him?"

Ashlena's face grew cold. The question he had just asked her was unthinkable, yet there was the chance she could live. What choice did she have? If she did not accept what he asked, she would return to where he had awakened her. If it meant finishing her life in the town of Oulhaven and having a somewhat normal life, then maybe it was worth it. It had to be worth it. The only other choice was to accept her death now. Maybe she could withstand it. Maybe it would not be fatal. After all, it had never happened before. Most importantly, how could she let down all life in Brendonia?

Then, as if coming out of a trance, Ashlena gave her answer: "Yes, I will bear the child for you."

Inside the Old Time Tavern, music and laughter drowned out the storm. Customers from the village of Celesta filled the well-known place on this particular night. Placed neatly around the room, wooden tables and chairs furnished the old tavern. On many of the tables sat small, unlit lanterns. In the back of the tavern, there was a beautiful fireplace blazing, giving off a welcoming warmness to the room. The large fire cast great shadows on the tavern's knotted oak walls. In front of the flickering fire gathered a group of minstrels, joyfully playing their soothing music to the people. Near the entrance was a long table stretching the length of the front wall. This was the bar. Several large barrels of ale were stocked behind the bar. In front of the barrels stood Evan, the owner, a man about five feet tall, dressed in a white tunic, covered by a brown leather vest. The man's head looked disproportionately large, even on his stocky body. His hair was dark brown, sticking up in some places, but fairly matted down in others. The man's face portrayed hard, thick-looking features including an unmistakably masculine nose.

"Evan, bring me my ale, you fat toad!" a large warrior wearing shiny armor and a powerful-looking sword and scabbard said playfully from a far corner of the room.

"Wait your turn, you overgrown horse," Evan shouted back smiling, "or I'll throw you outta here myself," the owner threatened. The big warrior and his small band of friends laughed loudly, thoroughly enjoying themselves. Evan opened the tap releasing a golden stream of ale, filling up the tin mugs one after the other. When the mugs were full, he closed the tap on the wooden barrel and walked toward the warrior's table. He thought about how he loved these stormy nights because they always brought good business. Evan walked over to his warrior friend in the corner and slid the mug of ale to him, "Here, ya ugly ox!" Turning and walking away, Evan smiled and delivered the other mugs to their tables.

It was then that the entrance door swung open, crashing against the ancient bulwark, the sound reverberating through the tavern's walls. The exuberant music died out on an off-key note. The lighthearted chatter of the room expired with a seething whisper. The storm intruded into the tavern, the rain pouring through the door soaking a section of the tavern's floor. As Evan turned around, he widened his eyes in surprise. In the doorway stood a huge man dressed in drenched, black robes; his face was completely cast in shadow by a ragged hood over his head. The giant stranger held a beautiful woman covered in blankets permeated with water. Evan went to the door, closing it tightly. Now the whole room was deadly silent. A few people started to laugh, breaking the tension in the room. The stranger walked to the bar and gently laid the woman down. The dark man reached up and lowered his hood revealing his mysterious face. Evan gasped looking into the stranger's glowing blue eyes. At once, the eerie light died out revealing two stern, black eyes. The man's face looked as if chiseled from stone, marred only by a flowing black beard. What one could see of the stranger's hands resembled the bark of a willow tree. Pantos had undergone a great change since he bonded with Ashlena. His once flawless beauty was now flushed away from his face. Hard, strict features formed the curves of his face, creating the appearance of old age. Even his robes were now shredded and torn, giving him an ominous appearance.

"May I be of service to you, sir?" Evan said kindly, not wishing to start any trouble.

"This woman is with child. Can any of you help her?" The tall man raised his voice making it sound as though it were not a question.

"I can deliver the child," a man said making his way through the crowd. "I am a doctor."

Evan stepped forward to protest, but stopped after seeing the villager's intent on examining the pregnant woman. The doctor was a normal-sized man with an older face. What little hair remained was either gray or white.

"May I ask your name?" the doctor asked as his thick-fingered hands worked quickly and efficiently examining her.

"Ashlena," she whispered in a weak voice that was difficult to hear.

"There's no time to move her. Evan, get me some blankets and warm water," the doctor ordered.

Evan, looking at Ashlena who seemed calm now, nodded and started to the kitchen.

Evan passed the edge of the bar and turned into the kitchen, which was a well-lighted room filled with his workers. They were yelling back and forth busily cooking orders, oblivious to the proceedings in the dining room. Below this clatter, the sizzling of spitted meat filled the room.

A piercing howl came from the dining area. Instantly, Evan ordered, "I need blankets and some warm water!" Within less than a minute, two of Evan's cooks arrived carrying a bundle of blankets and a dishpan of warm water. "Thanks. Now get back to work," was the last thing Evan said, thinking there was no reason to stop business. The cook had asked him about the screams; however, Evan was already out the doors approaching the dining room.

The small bartender trudged out of the kitchen carrying a cumbersome bundle of blankets, carefully balancing a pan of water on top. The people watching him quickly lost interest when the woman screamed a horrifying note. Ignoring the confused chatter of the people, Evan pushed his way through the dense crowd, which had gathered since his departure.

"Give him room," yelled the doctor. Evan broke through the crowd with the supplies, giving them to the doctor. The always-cheery bartender had a look of worry carved upon his face. To Evan, time passed slowly, and the screams of Ashlena just seemed to prolong the wait. Occasionally, Evan shifted his eyes to look at Pantos. The bartender assumed the two strangers to be husband and wife, but it was impossible to tell.

The mysterious man stood unmoving in a confined space, staring blankly at Ashlena. Evan could not be sure, but the man would often look about the corners of the room for some unknown reason or to make sure something was still there. It was almost as if the man was expecting someone else to be there.

"It's a boy," exclaimed the doctor, as the two front windows of the tavern blew open sending rain and wind forcefully through the tavern, scattering tables across the room injuring several people. The violent storm thundered, shaking the walls as if to rip the tavern from its very foundation. The rain soaked the inside of the old time tavern, extinguishing the once warm fire in the fireplace. At the very same moment the child took his first breath of life, Pantos was no longer his own master. The interference had taken place. His immortal friends were now his bitter enemies. His strong flawless body was now weak and twisted. Upon the child's second breath, Pantos' body was forcibly teleported among the gods for trial and punishment. The god had broken the only law of the immortals, that of intervention. Pantos vanished from the physical world of Brendonia as quickly as he had come.

Evan, desperately trying to reach the windows, rushed through the panic-stricken crowd. Men and women selfishly pushed toward the tavern's front door. Suddenly, the storm's fierceness became second to the earthquake that now shook the tavern and destroyed the front door.

Then a flash of lightning struck, illuminating the frame of the open doorway. People raced out of the tavern leaving dozens trampled dead on the wooden floor.

"Somebody light a lantern!" Evan screamed into the darkness, but there was no response.

Remembering the baby, he stumbled around the tavern listening for a cry. "Ouch!" Evan yelled as he tripped, only to fall on the hard, wooden floor. Then, stumbling to his feet, he kicked something he knew to be a lantern. The little man quickly picked up the lantern while at the same time he pulled a flint from his pocket. Finally, after a few disgusted tries, he ignited the lantern. He heard and saw the tin mugs and wood crashing on the floor from the earthquake's wrath. Evan caught a glimpse of something near the bar. It was the doctor lying dead, apparently trampled. A strange glow caught the bartender's attention. Evan swore he saw a pair of eyes glow fiery red in the corner of the room. As he went to confirm this, another quake shook the floor, followed by many unbelievable streaks of lightning shooting horizontally through the room sparking fires everywhere.

Seconds later, Evan saw what he believed to be another set of eyes, yet smaller, glow ocean blue in the same mysterious corner, perhaps the eyes of a child. The fire was now spreading uncontrollably, bringing vibrant light to the whole tavern. Evan saw that the mother was dead, and he could find no sign of the father. The entire tavern was empty. Only the dead remained. Not a sole person had stayed to help. Evan was alone. Hearing a cry, Evan swiftly turned his gaze to the mysterious corner, instinctively knowing the sound had come from there. He briefly glimpsed an image of a cloaked man holding a baby. But, before running to help them, he was forced to close his smoke-filled eyes, trying to diminish the stinging. When he reopened them, the corner was engulfed in flames, and the man and child were gone. The good-hearted bartender, realizing that they had perished, reluctantly ran out of the tavern.

The rain poured over Evan as he rubbed at his smoke-blackened face. The pudgy bartender stumbled helplessly to the ground. Exhausted, he wondered who had been holding the baby. Evan felt sure it was not the mysterious man who carried in the woman. No, it was someone else, but who? Evan raised his head, taking one last look at his beloved tavern, now in an uproar of flames. He began to faint in grief. Evan later swore that, in his last second of consciousness, he had seen a huge streak of fire shooting in a path across the ground into the forest, eventually extinguished by the flooding rain.

CHAPTER 1

GLANTIS TREFMORE

BRENDONIA'S RED SUN PEEKED from the horizon, bringing its soothing light to the world. All was quiet in lower Brendonia. Not a single animal stirred. Not many people rose from their beds to see the coming of dawn anymore. The unpredictable weather and the almost complete splitting of the continent fifteen years ago had produced an ever-worsening age of sorrow. It was now the end of winter; however, the season produced no snow or rain. The forest animals were extremely scarce. The people of lower Brendonia were beginning to worry. Strange things were happening to their world and no one, not even their king, had answers.

The sun barely reached the village of Celesta, its faint rays reflecting on the rooftops through the morning dew. As time passed, beams of sunlight began to penetrate through the once deep green trees in the Wood of Kinet where Drek Trefmore sat in his quaint home. The shadow-faced man drank a steaming liquid, strangely shivering as it went down his throat. Drek raised the tin mug and threw its contents into the small fire, completely extinguishing it. He pulled his long black robes around himself tightly in disgust. He looked out the window, his red eyes catching the weak rays of the sun. Even at its brightest, the sun's rays were no match for the mage's fiery eyes. Drek stood up and seemingly slid to the window, his feet covered under the lengthy robes. Drek stood an average height; however, his thinness and long robes created an illusion of tallness. He looked extremely frail, with hands so chapped that they appeared as if someone had painted them red.

"It is time to end this nonsense," Drek thought. "The boy is old enough now and must go on alone for a time. I've seen nothing of his powers. If they truly are locked within his body, then my babysitting is only hindering them from sprouting."

Drek drifted to his home's front door. He unlocked it, his hands unseen beneath his robe's sleeves. Drek pushed the door open and looked into the forest.

"Glantis," he called in a hoarse voice.

"Be right there!" The huge youth yelled back from the forest in a deep voice. Glantis Trefmore swung his axe in a vertical sweep splitting the dry wood in half. He stood up straight and leaned back stretching his tense, lower back muscles. "Ah, that feels better," Glantis remarked to himself. The powerful boy bent over and reached for the firewood. Glantis wore a pair of heavy black boots and a thick pair of brown pants. He wore a blue tunic with sleeves rolled just past his massive forearms. At only fifteen, he was huge for his age. The boy stood well over six feet tall, and his legs were thick with muscle. His chest and back together had a width thicker than most tree trunks.

It was a nice morning. The skies were clear and the sun shined freely. It was very cool outside, but it felt warm compared to the cold days of a normal winter. With spring just around the corner, not many chilling days remained, but these were only assumptions. Winter had produced no snow. The people of Brendonia could only hope that this was a quirk of nature. Everyone now waited patiently for spring, hoping the season's refreshing rains would shower upon the land.

Glantis grasped some firewood with his callused hands and began walking toward the house. "I sure have done a large amount of work on this house," he thought, staring at the newly built porch. Glantis stepped up onto it smiling as he heard the satisfyingly solid thud of his boots hitting the floor. Setting down the wood, Glantis swung himself around and stared into the forest. The sun reflected off his dark blue eyes causing him to squint. "What the…" Glantis both spoke and thought while scratching at his rugged brown hair.

"What is it, Glantis?" Drek said peering from the doorway.

"I don't know. I thought I saw an animal," Glantis replied in a whisper.

"What did it look like?" asked Drek appearing to be interested.

"I barely saw it, but whatever it was, it sure wasn't small."

"You better come inside. Animals can be vicious when looking for food these days," Drek said with intent. "Come inside, I need to speak with you."

Glantis reluctantly stepped inside while staring back into the woods, hoping to catch a glimpse of the large animal again. He finally gave up and shut the door. Glantis went to the corner of the room and set a log in the fireplace. He rekindled the fire, and it quickly warmed the two-room home. Glantis raised himself up from the floor feeling tenseness in his knees, having been on his feet since the early hours of morning. He started for his bedroom when Drek insisted, "Glantis, I wish to speak with you."

Glantis reluctantly turned around and went to sit at the table with Drek. "What is it?" he questioned, already knowing what it was. "Wait, before you say anything, let me speak without interruption." Glantis spoke seriously, his blue eyes locking with Drek's crimson eyes. "I realize that ever since I finished schooling in the village of Celesta you have been hinting that I choose an occupation. Well, I've chosen one. I've decided to go to Castle Brendonia. There I will join the king's army," Glantis continued, never looking away. Drek began to speak but stopped cold upon seeing Glantis' determined face. "And, as you probably know, I have come to realize that you are not my true father."

Drek began to protest, but Glantis gestured sternly.

"I have only seen you in your robes. I have never seen your face outside the shadows from within your hood. I can't tell you how many nightmares I've had about you. The only proof I have that you're human is that you walk on two legs and speak the native tongue of Brendonia," Glantis said in a cutting tone, never stopping for a breath of air. "All I've seen are those blasted eyes of yours, sometimes glowing red within the hood you wear. Since the first time you took me to Celesta, I knew I was different from the other kids. At first, it was just my size, and later I noticed the way you were raising me differed from the other children. As soon as school was out, you forced me to come right home. I had to learn to entertain myself with either books or things in the forest. I ask you, why? Why did you raise me in isolation from the other kids?"

Tension dominated the room. Neither spoke for a time. This was the first time Glantis had confronted Drek. While growing up, he had always wanted to know the reasons for Drek's strictness, yet until now, he could never bring himself to question Drek.

"I try to love you as my real father, and I feel your inner conflict. I see a certain suffering within you, and I sometimes wonder if it is related to me." Glantis spoke wisely, "I wish to ask something of you before I leave to join the Brendonian Legion."

There was another silent pause between the two.

"Ask as you will, Glantis," Drek broke the silence with a piercing whisper, an almost frightening sound.

"I know your power is strong, but I know not what it is. As you have told me, a great evil is spreading its arms around this land. I love Brendonia, and I will not sit idly by watching the trees wilt and the fields grow barren. No, that is why I want to join the king's army. I want to help fight off whatever this evil may be or help people in need that will surely suffer because of this ominous weather," Glantis paused in thought. He then added, "Something is wrong, and I want to help. I need a purpose in my life."

"I understand. What is it you wish of me?" Drek questioned, leaning forward in his chair.

"Help the people prepare for what may happen. Warn them. Convince them of the danger that you foresee." Glantis stared at his foster father.

"Someday, Glantis, I will tell you the story of your birth, for I do not even know your true parents. Something is very special about you that I cannot foresee," Drek said, feeling the old questions rising again in his mind as he recalled the stormy village night so long ago. "You, Glantis, are free to go wherever you wish, but be careful and know that your mind can deceive what's in your heart. As for me, I will travel to the village of Celesta tomorrow at dawn. It is not far, as you know having attended school there, but I feel I owe them a great favor, for they taught you well," Drek explained. "I can only enlighten the villagers of the evil. A warning is all of which I am capable. I have a good friend there who will spread my warnings to all the villages near Castle Brendonia. I am no diplomat, and the people will surely listen to him more than me. As you will learn, some people in this world only believe when it is too late." Drek paused in thought. "I leave you with this, Glantis. There is a reason for everything I did while raising you, but I have neither the authority nor the complete knowledge to justify my actions. Believe in yourself, Glantis. May the gods guide your journey," Drek finished, lifting himself from his chair and walking to the front door. Bidding Glantis goodbye with a motion, the mage slipped out of the home, already beginning his journey.

Glantis watched Drek leave the house. Getting up out of his chair and walking to his bedroom, he thought, "Strange he is, never sleeping, always leaving the house at night. Now he leaves on a journey, yet takes nothing. He leaves, yet his cold presence somehow remains here. Drek is a mere man in black robes, almost faceless to me, my caretaker. Why my father left me to this cold-hearted man, I may never know. What's stranger, I feel a kind of bond with him," Glantis thought, closing his bedroom door.

The bedroom was a small room without windows. Glantis walked over to a lantern in the corner of the room and lit it. Next, he went over to a large wooden cabinet and began to pack things he needed for his journey to Castle Brendonia. It was still morning, but he would need the rest of the day to gather things if he was going to leave at dawn tomorrow. Many unanswered questions still remained in his head, questions that no one he knew could answer. Glantis wondered if he would ever know his true parents. He could not help wondering for what purpose his parents would leave him in the hands of Drek. These types of thoughts preoccupied him ever since he could remember. Many nights did Glantis stir in his sleep because of these constant, unanswered questions.

Glantis had spent the whole day packing food and collecting the items needed for his journey. He now sat on the porch of his house, ending the day by sharpening his massive battle-axe. Glantis treasured this ancient axe. He had found it one evening, deep in the Wood of Kinet. He was only six years old then, and it had taken him hours to drag it back home. Glantis remembered getting a good scolding for getting home so late that night. Now it seemed worth the trouble, he thought, as he finished polishing the bright silver metal that shined in the moonlight. Glantis, admiring the strong oaken handle, could not help wondering to whom this magnificent axe had once belonged. Drek had said it was very old, ancient perhaps. He had never seen the likes of it before.

Wearily, he got up and went inside the house. Glantis retired to his bedroom. He would rise early the next morning. Drek had not returned since his early morning departure. He kept his word, so it seemed. He was probably somewhere in the forest on his way to the village of Celesta. Glantis pondered his choice in joining the Brendonian Legion. Slowly, he fell into a deep slumber, dreaming vividly of treacherous adventures and exhausting battles against faceless enemies.

Glantis rose early the next morning, the sun not yet breaking over the horizon. He ate a quick breakfast, gathered his things, and went out the front door. Just before he shut it, he retrieved his heavy battle-axe from the corner. Glantis then shut the thick wooden door of the house and secured the locks. He began to walk into the forest looking back only once, thinking how he would not be returning for a long while. Oddly, he was already missing Drek, despite him being more of a presence than a foster father. He trudged on, though, knowing it was time to go his own way.

The evening sun began to touch the western horizon, sending a beam of orange light through the forest. The usual haziness began to dissipate. The dark haze seemed to clear, allowing the sun's golden light to glimmer through the trees. Glantis walked through the woods, indifferent. The day had been cloudy and dismal, making the journey seem endless. The new light sparkling through the forest beamed upon him with a warming sensation.

"Great timing," Glantis thought sarcastically. He was glad the sun did come out, though. Its orange light made the forest so peaceful.

He stopped dead in his tracks. He had arrived at the edge of a small cliff just outside the forest. "So that's why the sun lighted this part of the forest so well." Glantis reached up and scratched his head. He had been so absorbed in his plans that he had not even noticed the forest's end. He looked down over the small cliff's edge. Squinting because the sun was so low it shined directly into his eyes. He brought his large callused hand up to his head and shaded his blue eyes from the bright rays. He stood silent for a long moment, frozen by the wondrous sight. Before him, several miles in the distance, sat Castle Brendonia. Glantis' strength instantly renewed as he looked upon this great structure. He gripped his pack tight and ran down the cliff with enthusiasm. As he descended, the sun began to fall behind the great castle. Glantis stumbled down the cliff, only to get up again to run across the grassland of the Brendonian Plains. He had only heard stories of the ancient castle and as a child rarely left his foster father's sight. He had read about and studied the castle many times at school in Celesta. Castle Brendonia was the supreme force in the land. Since the time of construction, its armies swept the land of evil. Several times did the armies restore the peace for all of Brendonia. Glantis had no idea that the castle was anything like this, so giant, so beautiful. No book did it justice.

Glantis began to tire from running through the tall grass with all his heavy gear. He began to walk the remaining distance. The castle stood only a few miles away from him.

"Yes," Glantis thought. His choice had been a wise one. He would learn much here. Glantis could now make out where the main gate was, noticing the two front towers on either side of the entrance. Far above the horizon line, the castle's towers stood blocking the sun's rays. Five great towers stood in all, each of them equal in height and size, located on the five corners of the castle, creating the castle's well-known pentagonal shape. He was getting closer now, and the details were coming into focus. He could now make out the actual size of the castle. It looked as though his over six-foot frame was no bigger than one of the stone blocks within the wall. Finally, he reached the wide road leading up to the castle. Glantis now faced the two front towers, seeing the giant iron doors that led into the impenetrable fortress. He surmised that this was one reason why Castle Brendonia had ruled the land for so long.

Glantis stopped himself for a moment to prepare. He was a little nervous about being an outsider. The only people he had ever interacted with were fellow villagers of Celesta. Drek neither had taken him to nor let him explore the world beyond the village. It was always schooling that mattered, Glantis recalled angrily. He was never allowed to participate with the other kids on trips to the castle to meet soldiers or get a lucky glance at King Hestin of Brendonia. Whenever Glantis questioned Drek, he would always get the same answer: "There are certain rules we both have to follow, Glantis." Glantis had never understood this, but he had learned to accept it.

He looked up, breaking his disturbing thoughts, took a full breath of air, put on his serious face and began walking toward the iron doors. Glantis knew it was best that he left Drek behind. He was on his own now. He was his own master. Despite everything, he had always felt different somehow. He hoped his future at the castle would help to reveal this mystery and give him a sense of purpose in life.

Glantis suddenly became aware of the sound of horses. He turned around, looking back down the long winding road. He saw a band of thirty to forty horses riding toward him. The sound of pounding hooves filled the once silent evening. The wide road seemed narrower as the band of horses drew near. The road behind the horses seemed to disappear as the steeds kicked up a dusty trail.

"They must be part of Brendonia's army," Glantis thought, watching the horsemen come into view. Just as it seemed the horses would be on top of him, a loud command echoed across the dull-colored grassland of the Brendonian Plains. Within a moment, all the horsemen brought their steeds to a halt. Glantis noticed some of the men were in armor, others in common clothes. These commoners were certainly not in the army. In the front sat a stern-looking man dressed in full armor. Next to him, another sat holding the crest of Brendonia. Glantis admired the crest for a moment. It bore two swords crossed to form an "x." He then looked back on the group of horsemen, formulating a question. This was definitely the army, but why were there common people with the soldiers?

"Where is your destination, boy?" the officer holding the crest bellowed.

"I am on my way to the castle," Glantis answered. "I have come to serve in the army and learn the ways of combat," he added.

The man holding the crest was about to say something when the rider next to him gestured not to. Glantis admired the authority of the man. He was obviously of a higher rank. His horse and armor were of top quality.

"What is your name, son? How old are you?" the man asked.

"My name is Glantis Trefmore, and I am of fifteen years, sir."

The man stared at Glantis pensively for a moment. "If you wish to join the army, so be it," the officer stated. "Vincent, put this boy on with one of the commoner's horses," the helmed officer said behind his visor.

"But sir?" protested Vincent.

"Do as I say, Vincent."

The disapproving soldier went to Glantis and escorted him roughly over to a mounted horse. Vincent felt the boy had the physical strength and size to be a soldier, but he was a fifteen-year-old. He was thinking only of the boy's good fortune. He was surely not ready for the discipline and brutality of army training, let alone an actual battle.

"Get up there, boy," Vincent said in an annoyed tone. He then looked up at Glantis. "Are you sure you're ready for this, son?"

Glantis saw the concern in the haggard warrior's face but could only nod in affirmation. Glantis mounted upon a horse with one of the commoners. As Vincent returned to his horse, the man with Glantis turned around and nodded in greeting.

"Yah," the commanding officer kicked his horse ordering it to move.

"That's odd," Glantis thought. According to school, one had to prove his worth to the army in combat. If done, you would receive the utmost respect. Soldiers would never set out from the castle to gather up men interested in joining the army. This could only mean one thing: the trouble that Drek had foreseen.

Once again, the man with Glantis turned and smiled as if sensing his nervous thoughts. He urged his horse forward and followed the rest of the group.

The sun had set as they entered the castle's imposing doors. Darkness spread across the plains. A chill came to Glantis' body as the dark doors closed behind him with a screeching sound, ending in a loud, echoing boom. He felt what he hoped to be winter's last chill. After the guards secured the doors, they led Glantis and the other men, at least fifty, through the huge entry yard. Here, they dismounted the horses. Within a few moments, several stablemen came out and led the horses down the left corridor to the stables. From what Glantis could see, the right corridor led to the inner town of the castle.

"This way!" the guards ordered, interrupting his thoughts. They were walking straight ahead to a set of doors. Upon reaching them, Glantis noticed Vincent and his commanding officer were gone. The guards unlocked the thick gold-trimmed doors, revealing a giant room. In front of them was spread a long blue carpet leading to a throne. It was the most magnificent thing Glantis had ever seen. He stood there looking, his mouth open like an astonished child. The room was made of gleaming white marble trimmed with gold. Hundreds of shiny wooden benches covered the floor on both sides of the room, probably used for large meetings between other races in Brendonia.

Several other guards that were already in the room came to the doorway. They surrounded the men, blocking their pathway with swords. One of the guards that brought them to the room was the only one let through. He moved along the blue carpet toward the throne where an old man sat. Dark eyes and a stern countenance offset his white hair and withered appearance. On either side of him stood a guard, along with several advisors wearing brightly colored garments, each bearing the crest of the Brendonian Legion upon their tunics. The throne was made of gold, and it was perched atop a platform reached by marble stairs. The guard walked up the solid marble stairs and kneeled.

"You may rise," the King of Brendonia said in a deep, garbled voice. The guard walked closer and whispered something in his ruler's ear. The king's face grew weary. He spoke back to the guard. The soldier stood up and bowed. He gestured to the other guard, prompting Glantis and the others to move. Then all the men in the group bowed. Glantis awkwardly followed, snatching another glance at the king. The group then moved back out of the room while two guards closed the throne room doors.

Again, they passed the corridor leading to the inner city and then went through an open archway leading down another hallway. This wide hall had several other halls intersecting it. As Glantis passed by, he noticed several doors on each wall, along with rows and rows of torches illuminating the walkways. Even with all the light, the castle remained in shadows. As much as he wanted to explore, the guards kept leading the group toward the back of the castle.

Finally, they reached the end of the hallway. Here stood another set of doors, this time made of wood, which appeared to be rotting. When the guards opened these doors, a rush of air blew through the hallway, chilling the men on this cold night. Astonished by the view beyond the doors, Glantis did not notice the cold. They were outside in what must be the army barracks, a huge area covered in grass. To the left and right were giant stone buildings. Three massive towers, one standing solely at the back and the other two placed slightly forward on opposite sides, formed a triangle. These great towers reached high into the night sky.

"All right, men," one of the armored soldiers spoke, breaking the night's stillness. "You have a long day tomorrow, so you better get a few hours rest," the guard laughed.

Glantis realized he was tired. All of a sudden, his pack and axe felt heavy on his broad shoulders. Quickly, the guards split the group in half, leading them to the stone buildings on the right and left of the inner courtyard. There were only about fifty men total, not at all a large number of new recruits. The guard opened the door and led them inside. "Pick a bed," the guard announced, locking the door tightly behind him as he exited the room.

CHAPTER 2

MYSTERIES FROM ABOVE AND BELOW

JUST BEFORE THE SUN ROSE in the village of Celesta, the loud ringing of a bell awoke the entire populace from their beds. Slowly, family groups promenaded out of their homes and began to fill the village square.

"What's the meaning of this? It's too early for a meeting," a man said while rubbing his tired eyes.

Shouts of confusion filled the once silent morning while the children began to play, running wildly around their distracted parents. People were yelling back and forth, hoping to find out what was happening.

At the front of the village square stood an exquisitely crafted podium, set upon a beautiful foundation of rock. Attached to it was a brilliant gold bell still humming from its last ring. Its purpose was to call village meetings, usually in times of vibrant revels or dire urgency. Alongside the bell towered Drek in his flowing black robes; the dark cloth periodically blocking the early morning sun from the people's sight. Standing next to him was a very old man wearing the robes of a holy man. This was the familiar village cleric, whose thin white beard matched that of his milky robes. They stood close together, upon the platform conversing, their colors neutralizing each other.

Suddenly, as if coming out of a trance, the white-robed cleric stepped over to the hanging bell. Grabbing the rope, he shook it frantically, producing a piercing tone. Immediately, the confused crowd fell into a silent murmur. As the bell's last tone faded, the cleric began to speak.

"People of Celesta, my good friend, Drek, brings some disturbing news. It seems the king is sending out his men each and every day to the many towns of lower Brendonia."

"So what, Tursophonie, this is not uncommon. The king periodically visits the towns in greeting," one person interrupted.

"I agree, my friend, but he is collecting men as well!" Tursophonie said in a cutting tone. "At this time, the king is bribing men with promises of wealth if they join the army. Drek feels certain that, in a few months, this will change and the king will be conscripting men by law. It seems the druids from upper Brendonia are getting land hungry again."

"How can we believe this friend of yours? Does he not wear the black robes?" a blacksmith shouted from among the gathered townspeople.

"Do not the druids wear this color?" another man bellowed from the crowd. This time, however, the village square filled with rumblings of agreement.

"People, please!" Tursophonie said, his face beginning to alter. "You all know of the fierce storm that long ago wrecked this village. You also know of the Brendonian continent sinking, creating a massive division that formed upper and lower Brendonia. Well, in case you haven't noticed, my friends, when that division occurred, our control over the druids went with it. Only the gods know what's in store for us. Who knows what they've done to the dwarven homes in the city of Lore. I predict soon that the peace between us will fail, if it already hasn't. We all know of the cultish druids that live within the Ancient Forest. If you remember, they weren't exactly overjoyed with the idea of being under the control of the king."

"Tursophonie, surely you can't prove any of this to be true. Just because the king is collecting men means nothing," a short, heavy-set man bellowed.

"Your point is well taken, but I doubt that you can prove it isn't true. All I ask is that you trust my friend's word and that you prepare yourselves for the problems that may or may not arise," the white-robed cleric said in a calming voice.

"We do not need to prepare for war. What we need is better hunting equipment," an old woman nagged from the crowd. "I can barely feed my child."

"Open your eyes! This winter season was completely devoid of snow. Can any of you remember when something like this happened? No, of course not. It has never happened before. Face it, my people. It is not the trapping equipment that is at fault, but the changed behavior of the animals. They have become more and more aggressive over the last few years. It's as if the animals sense something we do not. It is practically unsafe to travel in the forest, even in daylight," Tursophonie pointed out.

The people began to stir, throwing up their hands at the two men standing upon the platform. Men and women were yelling out comments about how Tursophonie must have read one too many books. Slowly, they began to return to their homes.

"Drek, my old friend, I am afraid the people will not listen. You must remember the village is just now forgetting the horrible disaster that struck many years ago, and they will not hear of war because war brings death. It will take more than us to convince them of the trouble brewing," Tursophonie said softly to Drek who nodded in acknowledgement. He patted his old friend on the back and began to leave, walking slowly toward the village's end.

"Drek," Tursophonie called out. "I will travel to the towns of Vwelton and Carst. Perhaps there I will get better results."

Drek smiled back at his friend, knowing that he would do his best. Drek, however, knew it was hopeless. He had seen the reaction of the villagers, blinded to everything that meant change, closed off to the possibilities of war. Little did they understand that to keep the peace one must sometimes fight.

As Drek reached the forest, he heard a distant, yet familiar screeching sound. All the townspeople began to look around at each other in bewilderment. Then another loud screech sounded, this time closer, attracting everyone's attention to the morning sky. People began to scream from all corners of the village. Within moments, everyone broke into a panic. Women grabbed their children by the ears and scurried into their homes. Some of the brave men unsheathed their swords and held them in a defensive position, while others strung bows, ready to fire at a moment's notice.

Drek stood alone in a clearing just outside of the village, watching the huge dark shape come closer. Now the tall trees began to sway from sudden bursts of wind caused by the huge beast's passage. Dust began to swirl, blinding everyone for a brief moment. Then they saw it, a huge orange bird with a wingspan close to fifty feet. It screeched, still airborne, circling above. Its feathers were rust colored, contrasted with a sharp yellow beak, capable of eating a man in two or three bone-crushing chomps. The bird's feet were jet black with talons as sharp as dragon's teeth. The people were stunned as they recognized the beast, an ocherous from Bolonwood Forest, an animal not seen in these parts for over thirty years, not since the time men rode them during the Boundary Wars. Hopelessly, men began to shake, dropping their weapons. There was no use fighting these birds of war, at least not by means of swords or arrows. Only a mage or dragon would have a chance at killing an ocherous and both were thought to be extinct. When the dragons had attempted to reclaim the land, it had been the ocherous birds that forced them back into the Fire Crypts. At that time, the ocherous had outnumbered the dragons by far, winning the battle by sheer force. Yet these birds were not evil, but neutral in manner and regarded with extreme caution.

Women and children began to scream as the gargantuan ocherous began to slowly descend in a clearing beside the village.

"Do you see anyone of interest, Levantia?" questioned King Hestin, from one of the great towers.

"Yes, the one in the black armor, I think you know him," Levantia said, looking down at the green courtyard with a look of mischief in her eyes.

"Ah, that one is Surlonthes, my son," the king answered in a dignified tone. King Hestin's face began to break into a proud look. "My son," he thought. "He has an excellent sword hand, destined to become a great warrior and king." Brushing away his thoughts, he said, "So you wish to train my son for the kingdom's special task force?" He asked the question, but both of them knew for some time that Surlonthes would be part of the Brendonian special task force. The prince had trained with Levantia ever since he was of age.

"Wait," interrupted Levantia, "look at that one," pointing a finger in another direction.

King Hestin reluctantly looked away from Surlonthes to the indicated position on the field. "I see nothing," the king said in a terse manner.

All Levantia could do was point and laugh. The king suddenly smiled at what he saw on the grounds where the army practiced.

Glantis Trefmore clumsily swung his sword back and forth, attempting to defend himself against the onslaught of one of the armored trainers. Glantis had no training in any sort of fighting, and it was showing in this test. Men began to stop their sparring to watch this monster of a boy stumble around in circles, wildly swinging his sword. They all began to smile and laugh, watching Glantis try to balance his weight against the swift blows issued from the trainer's sword. Glantis was cut all over, nothing serious, but enough to make him feel foolish. Hearing the laughter ring in his ears upset him.

Without warning, he charged the trainer, holding his sword cocked back. The trainer easily dodged the weapon. Unfortunately, Glantis was in a full swing and could not check the motion of the sword before it hit the wall. As the cold steel first bit into the stone wall, it looked as though it was shimmering with a pale blue light. The blade then sliced through the stone, creating a trail of blue sparks that caused everyone to blink. When they opened their eyes, they saw Glantis sprawled out on the ground, separated from his sword. As several men hurried over to help revive Glantis, Surlonthes called out something to the trainer.

"What is it?" the trainer asked, looking over to where Surlonthes stood. "You look as if you've seen a ghost."

"Look at this wall. He cut right through the solid stone wall, cut right through it!" Surlonthes repeated. "No sword can do that!"

The trainer kneeled down and carefully examined the slit in the wall, noticing that the sword had made a clean slice right through the stone. The edges of the gash were smooth like polished marble. The trainer and Surlonthes were speechless.

"Janestin," Levantia yelled from high above on the tower. "Bring me Prince Surlonthes and that other man to my training quarters by sunrise tomorrow."

Janestin nodded quickly, distracted by the slit wall. He promptly returned to his men.

Glantis regained consciousness later that night. He found himself in the boarder house resting in his bed. Glantis got up and began to clean the cuts he had sustained earlier during the test.

44

"Well," he thought, "I realize now why the Brendonian Legion is so hard to get into. They issue tests the second you arrive to see if you have any potential abilities." Glantis practically ripped his boots off, throwing them under his bed. He had failed today and feared being kicked out of the army. Glantis rolled back into his bed, thinking, "If I could've only practiced." He quickly drifted off into the comforting escapism of sleep.

"Glantis, get up," a hand reached down and shook him. Glantis opened his eyes, startled to see a stern-looking man dressed in full armor trying to grab him. "Wait, I am Surlonthes, from the other boarder house across the army grounds. Yesterday we were ordered to report to Levantia at sunrise, but because you were unconscious at the time, I thought I'd stop by and roust you."

Glantis, not yet fully awake, dressed himself and quickly gathered up all his belongings. He followed Surlonthes out the boarder house door. They walked across the grassy field where they had tested yesterday. Upon reaching the other side, they came upon the rotted wooden door that Glantis recognized from two days ago. Surlonthes opened the door leading Glantis down the familiar corridor. They made their way toward the throne room, only this time they took a left down a different hallway. At its end was another door. Surlonthes looked through his ring of keys. Finding the one he wanted, he unlocked the door, revealing the foot of a circling staircase. The two men climbed the stairs and opened the door at the top. They entered a large hallway veering to the right. Glantis reluctantly followed Surlonthes through another door.

"You look troubled," Surlonthes stated. "You need not worry. We are being honored for our fighting skills." Before Glantis could respond, Surlonthes had already entered. The walls of the room displayed various weapons and armor, each of excellent craftsmanship. The other contents in the room were two comfortable-looking beds, placed on the far side of the room. On the opposite side was an unlit fireplace.

"This is our new home," Surlonthes smiled.

Glantis looked around again wondering what he had gotten himself into by coming to the castle. This surely could not be a punishment. There must be some mistake. Had he heard him right? Honored? Glantis walked to one of the beds and put down his things.

Suddenly, the door burst open and a helmeted stranger in full armor knocked into Surlonthes, sending him crashing to the floor. Next, the man advanced slowly toward Glantis, who quickly armed himself with his huge axe and assumed a tentative, defensive posture. Instead of attacking, the perpetrator dropped his hands to his sides and began to laugh. It was a surprisingly feminine sound.

"So this is what I have to work with?" the stranger remarked, "Work, indeed." The stranger removed the helmet still chuckling.

Surlonthes picked himself up, joining the laughter as he recognized Levantia.

"I should've known," Surlonthes' voice softened.

Glantis stood in awe as he looked at this beautiful woman. She had light brown flowing hair, with two eerie green eyes. She was somewhat muscular and judging by her performance, very quick. Levantia was the same age as Surlonthes, but she was almost twice Glantis' age. Glantis began to lower his axe taking a deep breath. His face projected an embarrassing aura around him.

"I expected a better response from you, Prince Surlonthes," she remarked in disappointment. "And you must be the stone cutter I sent for?" The woman turned toward Glantis, whose face flushed red as he remembered his inadequate presentation with the trainer.

"Worry not, for you would not be here if I didn't think you had the potential to become a great soldier. I am Levantia." She looked upon Glantis' boyish face, searching deeply into his dark blue eyes asking, "What do you call yourself?"

Glantis, feeling Levantia's green eyes burn through him, hesitantly answered, "Glantis Trefmore." He slowly stretched out his arm, opening his huge hand in greeting. Levantia smiled and shook his hand, staring into his eyes. Glantis, beginning to feel uncomfortable, looked away. Levantia was extremely attractive. Somehow, she reminded him of some-one. She would be their new trainer. Levantia was going to teach them everything about combat. All the training would be more individualized compared to the other soldiers.

The next few months were very difficult. Levantia could work wonders with the swords as well as any other weapon. She was a strict teacher and demanded the utmost of the two men. Surlonthes caught on easily and enhanced his skills well beyond advanced, while Glantis was still a bit unbalanced and uncoordinated. Levantia persevered and Glantis was improving, but slowly. Surlonthes sparred with him, but it was to no avail. Glantis would just become frustrated with his lack of skill. He could never loosen his grip on the sword. When he did, the sword would usually end up ten feet away on the floor. Nothing seemed to be working right. Glantis had the physical strength, yet he was lacking the coordination and mental determination due to his young age and huge body. He began to worry about what he would do if he did not improve. What would he do then? Would he return to his home? What would Drek think? He asked himself these questions repeatedly. He began to wonder about his parents. What kind of life would he have had with them instead of Drek, a man who raised him under strange rules that he himself could not justify. What of his ordeal on the training grounds? How did he manage to cut through that stone wall? Even worse, he did not remember doing it. Glantis took all these thoughts and buried them deeply within himself. He had not the time to deal with them now. Learning how to use various weapons was all that mattered now.

One night Glantis heard the prince and Levantia talking about the honors tournaments, which coincided with the end of all the warriors' training. These were the sparring battles at which warriors of any level had the opportunity to prove themselves worthy of advancement before the king. Only the top-ranking fighters would gain honor and earn officer status. The high point of the tournament was when the overall winner would spar with one of Levantia's students. Winning did not matter. It was how well the warrior utilized the techniques just learned that earned him the honor of being asked to join Levantia's special force, which directly served the king.

"Surlonthes," Levantia spoke seriously. "You are an excellent student. Over the years, I watched your training. I always knew when the time was right you would make an excellent soldier. I have chosen you to spar with this year's winner in the tournaments. I am afraid Glantis would shame the king and himself. He's just not good enough now. As I expected, he's just too young for his body. He hasn't had the training you've had all your life. Tomorrow I will break the news to him. His only chance to fight in the tournament this season will be from the lowest level, like all the other men," Levantia said with sorrow. "There's nothing more I can teach him. It's up to him now. When I first saw him, I thought there was some potential. Something seems to occupy his mind, as if it were not yet under his own control. I wish we could unravel the mystery of that first day when he cut that stone."

"The fact remains that we may never know what happened that day," Surlonthes stated. "It's his huge size that defeats him, and he's still too young. Why Janestin brought him here in the first place, I'll never know."

"Prince, even you know the answer to that. We are desperate for men. The army's been becoming sparser ever since Brendonia almost split in two."

"This is true, Levantia. Let's just hope that there's something to this boy's magical display in the courtyard. My father wants him under special surveillance. Indeed, these are strange times."

That conversation echoed in Glantis' mind. He was extremely depressed the whole night. He was ashamed and disappointed in himself. He wanted Levantia to be proud of him. Although he never knew his mother, she somehow reminded him of something lost. What was it that was bothering him? Was it his past, present, or future? Glantis noticed he was different from the others. He was crying and feeling sorry for himself. Glantis was fifteen years old, but he neither felt nor looked like any young boys he knew. That night, Glantis vowed that he would win that tournament, now only five days away.

He would begin to grow more mentally mature into his already giant shell of a man. Something inside of him was about to show itself, something that would change his whole life.

The following morning, Levantia began explaining to Glantis her decision about the tournament, although before she could finish, Glantis told her he no longer considered himself her responsibility. He told her he understood that he was not as good as she had hoped. Glantis thanked her, shaking her hand with a smile. He said he would fight in the tournament with the other men in order to prove himself. Glantis thanked Levantia again, gathered his possessions, and made his way down the hall toward the boarder houses. He had made the conversation a quick one, wanting to bother her no more.

"Glantis, wait." She stared at him, her beautiful green eyes becoming moist, sensing his deep disappointment. Her maternal instinct seemed to surface out of her soldier's body. She remembered that Glantis was younger than she had expected him to be. Having no words to comfort him, she said, "Take this sword and practice."

Glantis grasped the sword and left without a word. Levantia was all alone in the room.

The days went quickly as Glantis practiced. He could not forget Levantia's sad face when he left. In his eyes, he had disappointed her. Day after day, night after night, Glantis trained with the sword. He combined everything she had taught him and utilized it to the best of his ability. Soon his balance began to improve. He became consistently quicker and more accurate. Something was changing inside him. His concentration improved, self-correcting his every mistake. As Glantis became more relaxed, he and the weapon became one. Even in his sleep, he went over his every move and meditated on his victory at the tournament.

"Why have you summoned me here?" the mage asked in a whisper.

"I have seen it," the mysterious voice answered.

"Seen what?" the mage questioned wrapping his robes about his thin frame.

"I saw him use his powers on the castle wall," the voice explained.

"How did it come to be?" the mage walked closer to the speaker.

"He was training against another man. Others ridiculed him because of his clumsiness. His temper reached its maximum, and he swung his sword hard, missing his target. The blade shimmered with a blue aura and sliced the stone wall in front of him like it was made of water," the voice repeated what it had seen.

"You were right, then. Glantis has powers," the mage smiled, finally knowing the truth. He had not raised the boy the way he did for nothing. It was true. Glantis was Brendonia's hope against the evil that was sickening the land. The stranger, Pantos, that came to his home was indeed a god.

Suddenly, the present voice stabbed into the mage's thoughts like a knife. "Drek, you must go quickly. He's in danger!"

"Where is he?" Drek rasped in a frightening tone.

"Somewhere in the Wood of Kinet, save him, for he is the only thing capable of protecting our world from the powers of evil. Go!" the voice commanded. "Use your powers!"

"But—"

"I know you were sworn never to reveal your magic to Glantis, but the time is now. The god, Pantos, gave me authority to make this judgment. Go! You waste time!"

Drek went swiftly out of the valley, only to hear the speaker. "Protect him, Drek. If you're not too late, bring him to me, for I must enlighten him of his purpose. As you know he has many questions, all which I must do my best to answer as Pantos had entrusted me." The voice faded into silence.

Drek had little time before Glantis would be no more. "Pantos, he had called himself." Drek remembered the name as if he had always known it. When Pantos came to him, it was in a dreamlike mist. The only things he strongly recalled were the magnificent child and the instructions to care for him. He remembered no discussion of the matter.

After Pantos' vision had vanished, Drek had appeared inside the Old Time Tavern in Celesta Village. The next moment the child was in his arms and the tavern was in flames. In that brief second, he had magically transported himself out of the dangerous tavern, and to this day, Drek had no idea how he had done it.

"A tribute to the strongest army in all of Brendonia!" called out King Hestin to the crowd from the highest tower in Castle Brendonia. The people threw flowers toward the king's army as wild cheering echoed off the castle walls. Men, women, and children came from all the surrounding towns. This tournament was held every year, and this year it was especially welcome. It was a relief from all the strange weather and scarcity of animals. The people used it as an escape from all their worries and sorrows. "We are all gathered this spring day to recognize these brave men that have sworn an oath to honor and protect our kingdom," the king announced.

The people cheered again, expressing their feelings. The soldiers stood in long rows side by side, wearing their battle armor. All but Surlonthes wore the same rank. He had already proven himself on the testing grounds as elite. He had learned from Levantia, one of the best weapon experts in all of Brendonia. The others gathered today for one reason: to earn their rank. Thousands of soldiers stood along the castle walls cheering the new men that were about to compete in the tournaments. Despite the times, the army looked a bit healthier than in years past.

Glantis stood silently, listening to every word the king said. He was planning his every move in the tournament. The object of these games was to duel with swords or some other weapon. To win the match, you could either disarm your opponent or simply knock him off balance, thus putting him in a vulnerable position. During these games, it was common to get hurt. In rare cases a death might occur. Slipups or failure to parry a simple attack were extremely dangerous.

"I declare, by Brendonian Law, these games open!" Hestin's voice broke out in a familiar cry, piercing Glantis' thoughts. The people began to cheer as one by one the soldiers lined up around the grass-covered arena. The king sat back in his chair upon the rear tower of the castle. This year's games had about half the competitors than most years. Men were not joining the army, but rather staying with their families. This bothered the king. He remembered the last time this happened. It was during the Boundary Wars. He was young and his father was in power. Then, too, did the army's recruits become scarce. King Hestin remembered what his father had said to him hours before he was killed in battle, "Son, a king can only rule his people by first leading his people."

The day was long and hard for Glantis. Fight after fight he slowly climbed his way through the ranks. He had beaten everybody in the lower classes and had achieved, along with several others, the ranking of a commander in the army. This was an honorable position. It made a warrior one of the king's council members, wherein he would contribute to the discussion of war maneuvers. Glantis' age would still hold him back, of course, but his skills were honored. Glantis knew he had impressed everyone, including Levantia, but he was not satisfied. It was not enough that he bested so many men older than him. Still confused and yet excited for his victory and newfound skills, Glantis' enthusiasm caused him to get ahead of himself.

"Levantia, I challenge you to a game," Glantis spoke seriously, his voice cutting through all others.

The whole arena fell silent as the crowd realized Glantis' request. After a short moment, the king spoke. "Glantis Trefmore, no one has ever challenged the commander of my armies. It is foolish to ever think you could—"

"—Wait," the king was cut off by the voice of Levantia. "I accept the challenge, on the condition that I choose the weapons. If his majesty allows it, of course," she both bowed to the king and spoke firmly, hiding her smile of pure satisfaction.

The king smiled, "I will allow this challenge!" The crowd roared in agreement.

"Choose!" Glantis called to her over the cheering spectators.

"We will fight with these wooden quarter staffs," Levantia answered, handing one of the poles to Glantis.

King Hestin laughed aloud, remembering his own and Levantia's love for bravery and competition.

Glantis circled Levantia watching her every move, trying to anticipate her attack. Quickly, Levantia lunged forward swinging her staff toward Glantis' head. He easily blocked it, for it was a slow attack.

"She obviously is not trying," Glantis thought. This made him laugh to himself, knowing what he was going to do. The two staffs smashed together back and forth. Glantis kept swinging and blocking, forcing her into a corner. Then with one swift swing, Glantis broke her staff into two pieces. Levantia was caught off guard and surprised at his newly acquired skill. Glantis began to back up and stood in the center of the arena, knowing he could beat her with his size and strength advantage.

"It's not over yet, Trefmore!" Levantia called out. She charged him with two shortened staffs as weapons. Glantis instantly raised his staff in defense, but suddenly she was gone. The only thing he saw was two sticks lying in front of him. He realized the trick. Levantia had flipped over him, dropping the sticks as she jumped. As Glantis turned around, he was too late. She quickly disarmed him and kicked Glantis to the ground with her boot. The match was over.

"Welcome back, Glantis Trefmore," she laughed extending her arm and grabbing his hand. Pulling him up, she boxed his ears lightly. "I'm very proud of you."

Blushing, Glantis smiled knowing he was back in the special fighting group. All the people, even the king himself, stood up clapping at the wondrous show of arms. As King Hestin clapped, he remarked to his son, Surlonthes, how amazingly this young boy had fought. Surlonthes nodded, waving to Levantia with stars in his eyes. "Father, someday I hope to marry Levantia."

"I know, son, but these are not things to be discussed now. We have a kingdom to protect. Look at the men that fought today, below average fighters at best. These are surely grave times when one of the better soldiers of the Brendonian army is a mere boy. A large one, at that," the king tried to smile.

"Indeed, there are troubled days ahead of us, father."

The next morning a messenger came to Glantis' barracks. He told him that the king wished to see him. The man led Glantis down through several corridors, unlocking and locking doors as they walked. Soon they reached a beautiful, wooden door ornately trimmed with gold. The guard knocked and the king bid Glantis to enter.

"Yes, Sire," Glantis said, closing the heavy door tightly behind him. Inside he saw that the king had also called for Surlonthes and Levantia. The four of them were now alone.

The king broke the silence. "Glantis, you are a brave warrior and I would be honored to have you on my side. Yet I want you to know what you're up against. Soldiers are sometimes sent to complete many perilous tasks. It isn't always the glory you see at the castle. And there is the issue of your age...among other things unexplained..." the king trailed off.

"My King," Glantis replied. "I understand the dangers, but I will not stand idly by to watch my world be destroyed by the danger that comes."

"Sadly your assumption is right. I already have some of my top men looking out for any ships that might be sailing toward the castle. I fear war with the druids of upper Brendonia. They never liked being under my control when the continent was whole. Now I fear they have grown strong and are planning an attack. We've sighted druid ships in the New Sea, yet mysteriously they seem to vanish or perhaps just turn around. You see, when the continent partially split, my control over and communication with the dwarves and druids of upper Brendonia ended. Only the gods know what those two races have done to each other. It was foolish of me not to send ships over immediately after the continent almost broke apart. I took the easy path by pretending the two races would settle with each other. The dwarves were never great allies of ours, but that is no excuse. I sometimes wonder what is happening to some of my dwarven friends.

Now I cannot even get a ship there. The ships never return, and no message is received of their arrival or whereabouts." The king finished, oddly staring out the room's window. Then he spoke again in an emotionless voice. "You are all granted leave from the castle, if desired. And, Glantis," the king paused, "look into yourself. See if you can figure out where that power came from. I have seen many things in my time, dragons, magic, but I've never seen magic to be so strong in a boy. If I knew of any mage in this world, I'd take you to him. Alas, until I saw you, I thought magic a lost art, gone from the world. Take care of yourself, Glantis, and do not go far. We will need you." The king bid Glantis to leave.

CHAPTER 3

GOLIS AND THE FORESTS OF BRENDONIA

GLANTIS WALKED BRISKLY along the path leading away from the castle doors. He had been at the castle for a few months, and he felt homesick. In that time, he had learned to use many weapons in hand-to-hand combat, although he still favored his battle-axe. He smiled, remembering his first fight with Levantia. Glantis readjusted his pack and turned off the path toward the Wood of Kinet. He could not wait to get home, yet at the same time, he wanted to spend time with his new friends at the castle, above all Levantia. He had never felt safe in his whole life. Being around her reminded him of the mother he never knew. How that was possible, he did not know. All he knew was that she made him feel comfortable. He smiled when he thought of Surlonthes and her together. She would make a great queen someday, perhaps.

The sun just began to peek over the forest's edge, shining brilliantly on the grassy plains that surrounded the castle. Something seemed wrong, for the forest and the plains seemed dry. As Glantis climbed the steep cliff that marked the forest's end, he noticed the ill-looking trees. He had great difficulty getting over the small cliff because of the very dry, loose dirt. Finally, he reached the top and sat to rest. Glantis had spent most of the spring training at the castle. In those few months, it had not rained once. Strange things were happening to the land: a winter without snow and now spring without rain.

After traveling several miles, Glantis had decided to take a quick rest among some trees in the forest. When he woke up, he cursed himself for sleeping so long. The rest felt good, yet it was now evening. He only had a few hours before nightfall and would probably have to move fast to reach his home in time. For the next few hours, Glantis quickened his pace. Unfortunately, it was getting dark fast; reluctantly, he decided to stop and make camp. He started a fire and began to cook the choice meat he had gotten from the castle's larder.

The cook had given it to him as a tribute for his bravery at the tournaments.

Glantis sat still, anticipating his cooked meat. Over three hours had elapsed since he had eaten anything, and the smoke-dry smell was inviting. He had journeyed well over twenty miles trying to reach his home on the outer edges of the Wood of Kinet. He had hoped to travel through this forest before nightfall. Glantis shook his head, swearing in disgust. He still had another ten miles to cover. While smothering the vibrant cooking fire, he finished off his last piece of meat. The night felt cold and damp, and the chilling air easily penetrated the warrior's huge cloak. Glantis crunched up in his cloak, lying down next to an oak that towered over him. Just as sleep began to set in, he heard an eerie, rushing sound of wind. He stared into the blackness of the forest, straining his eyes, but saw nothing. With a sudden whooshing sound, a large, winged animal came swooping down from the great oak tree. This shadow of an animal plunged its claw into Glantis' muscular leg. Glantis shrieked out in horrifying pain. The warrior stumbled to his feet, clenching his powerful battle-axe from beneath his pack. He swung with one arm and hit the beast, tasting death in his eyes. The creature fell deadly silent. Glantis, noticing the body, recognized the animal to be a treefringe, a normally docile and harmless animal.

Suddenly, all the trees around him began to rustle, but this was not the wind as he had hoped. Black shadows began to pour out of the great oaks, gliding smoothly to the ground about him. Glantis limped away from the trees only to find himself surrounded by the hungry monsters. He lifted his axe and spun around slowly looking for his first attacker. His leg was bad. The throbbing pain and loss of blood were making it unbearable to stand. Glantis began to feel dizzy, but his adrenaline revived him as one of the treefringes attacked. The hissing animal swung his claw just scratching Glantis' massive right arm. Outraged, Glantis charged at the shadow smashing it out of the way with the flat of his axe. He then rearmed himself and took another swing, this time decapitating a second beast. Glantis had broken the circle, only to find two more treefringes drop down in front of him. They were definitely hungry and would not be scared off. Glantis blinked, looking at their bloodthirsty eyes. Dizziness overtook him, and Glantis began to collapse. A fierce growling awakened him as a large, four-legged animal toppled the two in front of Glantis, virtually tearing them apart with salivating jaws. Seeing this, he fell to the ground dropping his axe.

Out of nowhere screeched a huge bird as it swooped to the ground killing several beasts with its beak as it landed. Glantis strained, holding his neck up, staring at the black-robed figure dismounting the giant bird as he fell into unconsciousness.

Drek Trefmore watched in horror, seeing Glantis surrounded by treefringes. The black shadows began setting up their final killing stroke. Drek's eyes began to light up in an orange-red blaze as he raised his flaming hands. In an instant, all the treefringes lit up in orange flames that were impossible to put out. Then nothing, all was quiet. The treefringes deteriorated into piles of ash. Drek stared in shock as he turned his attention to a vicious pyren licking Glantis' pale face. It growled at Drek but stopped once it sensed he was there to help.

Drek walked over to Glantis, searching out his wounds. He found the deep crevice in which the claw had entered Glantis' leg. Drek immediately tore off a strip of cloth from his black robes. He lowered one of his bony hands to Glantis' leg, attempting to cauterize the wound.

"Be strong, my boy," Drek whispered as he placed his flaming hand upon the gushing wound. Glantis shuddered as Drek quickly removed his hand and covered the gash with the black cloth. Next, he literally lifted Glantis off the ground without strain and carried him to the giant bird. Even the great ocherous seemed shocked as his friend lifted the 250-pound body on his back. Not noticing his bird-friend's stare, Drek mounted the ocherous. The pyren started howling.

Drek stared at the tan-colored animal. It was definitely a pyren. Drek could tell it was just a pup, yet its size was tremendous. "Why did this beast protect Glantis?" Drek questioned himself, staring at the furry creature. The mage locked eyes with the pyren, attempting to scare it off with his glowing eyes. Surprisingly, the beast did not move or even flinch. Drek smiled, bringing his hand to his chin.

"It looks as though we've gained a friend, Plolate," Drek laughed while scratching the ocherous' neck feathers. Drek gestured the furry pyren to hop up on Plolate. Playfully, the tan beast leaped up on Plolate's orange-feathered back. Drek reached back his hand to pet the soft animal but quickly retracted it when the pyren growled, turning to lick Glantis' face. Drek laughed aloud, shaking his head in bewilderment as Plolate flew high into the sky. It seemed the ocherous' appearance would not be the strangest thing to happen this year.

"Southwest, as fast as you can, great bird, to the outer ridges of the Valley of Soul!"

Plolate descended into the Elven Forest in a tight clearing among the dense trees. Glantis began to wake as the morning sun brightened the green trees.

"Drek, it was you on that great war bird."

Drek nodded, smiling at Glantis. "Yes, Plolate. He is an old, old friend of mine." The bird screeched in affirmation.

"Funny," Drek thought, "he lost a good amount of blood, yet he has recovered in such a short amount of time. I would have thought he would've needed a few days' rest."

"By the gods," Drek broke out of his thoughts. "Glantis, you're walking!"

Glantis stood, not understanding Drek's words. Suddenly, he remembered the treefringe and quickly tore the bandage off his leg. Glantis stared at the wound then looked up at Drek. "My wound is…gone."

Drek bent down and looked for the wound. He rubbed his hand along the spot and found nothing as if it had never happened.

"This truly must be a gift from the gods," Drek whispered while looking up at the sky thinking of his first encounter with young Glantis. "There is no doubting it now," Drek thought. "He definitely has an unseen power."

Drek found himself wondering about Ashlena, the woman who gave birth to Glantis. Why had the immortal, Pantos, chosen him to raise the child before it was born in the tavern? Surely, there were others more capable and loving than he. Drek brushed the thoughts away, knowing that he himself would probably never know the answers. Just like Glantis, there were mysteries in his life. The matter was temporarily shut away in Drek's mind as a playful pyren knocked Glantis to the ground, licking his face.

"Where did he come from?" Glantis laughed, closing his eyes against the pyren's wet tongue. He then kneeled up, holding the playful animal down. "Wait," he said, cutting off Drek's reply, discovering the answer for himself. "This was the animal that attacked those two treefringes."

Drek nodded with his back turned toward Glantis.

"Drek," Glantis said in a changing tone. "What became of those beasts that were attacking me?"

"Let that be a question for Golis," Drek answered blankly.

"Who is that?"

"Golis is the master of the forests." There was a slight pause. Only the wind's crinkling of leaves sounded.

Glantis felt uneasiness in the air. "Why have you brought me here, and how did you find me?"

"A few days ago I was summoned by the forest master. He told me that you are, by fate, the one person that can help."

"Help, how?" Glantis asked.

"Yet another question I cannot answer. Old legends speak of a mortal man that can enter the valley without the admittance of the forest master himself. Golis feels you are that man," Drek finished looking into emptiness. The legend was true, yet Golis was using it as a test to see if Glantis was what Pantos said he would be.

"What happens if I cannot enter this valley?"

"You will never find it."

As Glantis was about to speak, Drek quickly cut in, "Go, Glantis. Go find the valley. Follow your instincts. You have only a few hours."

Glantis laughed sarcastically aloud as he gathered his things and walked into the forest away from their small camp. Enthusiastically, the great pyren began to run behind Glantis. Glantis stopped, smiling at the big, tan pyren. The animal was very large; however, Glantis knew it to be just a pup. Pyrens weighed as much as 800 pounds, due to a dense muscle structure and extreme bone mass. This one was roughly 150 pounds, extremely young. The pyren still had its baby teeth, very small, but razor sharp. Despite its present size, the animal was capable of killing just about anything, and with a life expectancy of sixty human years, it was obvious not many other land animals dominated its species. Glantis wondered why it had even strayed from its pack at such a young age. The pyren looked around one year old.

"We are very much alike, abandoned and alone at a young age. I shall give you the elven name 'Oonic' since you're known only to befriend elves." Glantis smiled. "In elven language I am quite sure 'Oonic' means 'follower.'" Oonic barked in recognition, or it seemed so.

Glantis and his new companion tramped through the forest, searching for the Valley of Soul. It was almost midday, and there was no trace of an open valley. The densely packed forest was a suitable home for the elves who loved it so. His time was almost out, but Glantis did not seem to care. He was already sick of the strange things Drek was telling him. At this point, Glantis just wanted to have a normal life. He had no idea what was happening to him and, in truth, he did not really want to know.

"We're not going anywhere," Glantis said smashing some thick brush with his axe. Oonic barked in agreement, rubbing his cold nose against Glantis' leg. "I know, I'm tired, too," Glantis said reaching down, scratching behind Oonic's furry ears. As he looked up, he saw a small opening between two trees.

"That wasn't there before," he thought. "Yet, I recognize this place because we just passed it." Glantis stood up slowly, holding up his axe. He began to walk toward the mysterious, black gap. As he moved closer, it appeared not to change, as if it was a wall. Again, he moved in closer, until he stood directly in front of it. First, he stuck his axe through the black void. When he put his foot through, it disappeared in the black hole. Bravely, he stepped through, gasping at what stood in front of him. He quickly jumped back out as if he could not breathe behind the wall.

"This isn't possible," he spoke looking up at the night sky, as if speaking to the gods above. "Oonic, look," Glantis pulled on Oonic's neck fat. Oonic began to growl, pulling back in a forbidding way. Glantis saw the fright in his eyes and let go. He kneeled down and began petting the pyren's beautiful, tan coat.

"I understand, my friend. Go back to camp if you think you can find it. I will be fine." Oonic got up on two legs, hesitated, barked, and then ran off. Glantis watched the pyren speed off into the distance, easily maneuvering over fallen trees and branches. As Oonic vanished, so did Glantis through the black wall. Once again, he looked in astonishment. It was extremely bright on the other side of the wall. "How?" Glantis thought. "All this light, yet, no sun." The whole place was a green valley covered in the greenest grass imaginable. Glantis had to squint at first because of the change in lighting. Eventually, his blue eyes began to adjust accordingly.

"By the gods," Glantis whispered looking down into the valley where a gigantic tree stood. It looked three times as thick as Castle Brendonia's walls, and its top stretched endlessly up into a glaring sky of white light. Its magnificent branches extended in all directions, never ending, only disappearing into the thick, white sky. The tree's color was the deepest, richest brown. The trunk of the tree was flawless.

"Please, come closer, Glantis Trefmore," a harmonic voice echoed.

Glantis swung his head around looking in all directions. He had heard something, yet not with his ears.

"My foster father, Drek, has sent me to find the forest master, Golis. If you are him, show yourself!" Glantis spoke in a serious tone, trying to hide his fear.

"I am," were the next words that burst into Glantis' mind.

"Something is speaking to me in my thoughts," Glantis said to himself.

"Yes, it is the only way I can communicate," the voice answered in Glantis' head.

"What are you?" Glantis asked.

"I am the great oak tree that stands before you, Glantis Trefmore."

"How is it you know my name?" Glantis pressed. "How is it you know my foster father, Drek?" he added. "How is it you—"

"—Come closer," Golis cut in. "I will answer all your questions, for I have much to tell you."

Glantis walked across the green valley toward the magnificent tree.

"Let me tell you a little story about your foster father, Drek," the voice spoke.

Hearing that, Glantis listened intently, extremely curious to what Golis would say about Drek. He was sick of the mystery surrounding him.

"He was once a very mischievous boy. He loved to fiddle with things. One time he stole an ancient talisman his father had found. Not knowing the danger of the talisman, Drek put on the old necklace. Unfortunately, for your foster father, the talisman was of dragon make. You see, for dragons, this magic enabled them to breathe fire, although when Drek invoked the talisman by placing it around his neck, it affected him differently."

"I thought dragons were born breathing fire," Glantis stated.

"My boy, the dragons are not just animals. They are far more intelligent than imaginable. The dragons of old had the ability to work magic. Thus, they constructed the talismans to enable all the dragons of the present and future to breathe fire. You see, only a rare bloodline of the dragons had the ability to work actual magic."

"Then why can Drek work magic? After all, he is human, isn't he?" Glantis wondered.

"He can only use the magic because of the talisman. It is not common for humans to even think about touching a dragon object, let alone invoke it."

"What exactly happened to him?" young Trefmore asked.

Golis continued his telepathy. "The magic was so strong that it burned away vital parts of Drek's soul. His innermost thoughts and essence of all he knew rapidly deteriorated. Only the one with the purest soul can enter my mythical valley without my consent. Yet, Drek found this valley one night after saving an ocherous from a small group of dragons tracking it. Drek helped the bird escape by sending up a wall of fire. The dragons didn't know that the wall of fire was harmless to their scales. Nevertheless, astonished by the sight of a human using magic, the dragons dared not to fly through it. Magic was an art lost many centuries ago by the human race."

"Plolate?" Glantis stared at Golis.

"Yes, did you think it was normal to ride those birds? The ocherous only tolerate men if it's to their advantage, like in the Boundary Wars when their very homes were threatened by every race upon Brendonia, including the dragons," Golis explained, pausing. He then continued to explain about Drek. "When Drek found me, he was a twisted, diminishing frame of a man, desperately seeking help. Seeing the good in him when he saved the ocherous, I allowed him to enter the valley, and I gave him the knowledge to regain his soul. That, my boy, is another story only he can tell. To this day, I know not what power the mage wields. Even now, Drek's innermost body has been twisted and turned into the element of fire by ancient dragon magic."

"Then why is it *I* can enter this valley?" Glantis looked skyward, watching the tree's branches spread into a white haze.

"Your real father was a god, your mother a human." There was a slight pause. "You, Glantis Trefmore, are a demigod, hereby the first to ever walk the plains of Brendonia. What could be more pure than a man that was half god? Pantos, your real father, saw the cruel future of the land and intervened by having a child that would be born to balance good and evil. Fifteen years ago, the night the center of Brendonia crumbled, Pantos came into my valley. He spoke of what was happening with the druids and what he proposed to do about it. I agreed to help the demigod child and direct him in the way your father Pantos had instructed me. He had already instructed Drek on your care. Pantos had decided that Drek would be your caretaker, or foster father, as you say."

"Master Golis, how did you know I actually existed?" Glantis asked.

"Drek was told to bring the child to me for further instruction of your care. So you see, Glantis, I am just another messenger for you, nothing more than a pawn to help you understand your reason for being here."

Glantis turned away from the tree in astonishment and discomfort. "Then why didn't Drek tell me these things as you have?"

Golis' voice softened. "Pantos had not revealed the full truths to Drek, in fear that he might become too cluttered with ideas and assumptions. The only instruction Pantos gave him was how to raise you. Most of what Drek knows is unconscious, and he knows only certain things I have told him. His role may seem small in all this, yet it was vital in your growth and development."

"Why was I raised by Drek rather than you in this untouchable valley?" Glantis asked turning around to face the forest master.

"As I've told you, Drek was instructed to raise you a certain way, a way that was placed into his mind by a god. Only Pantos understands its workings and affects on you. I, being an oak tree, could never have raised you in such a complex manner."

"Why did he go to all this trouble? Why didn't he just raise me himself?" Glantis asked with strong emotion, wishing his real father loved him enough to raise him.

"I can sense your feelings of abandonment. Your father had no choice in the matter. For him, it was the only way. At this very moment, somewhere, he is serving a severe punishment for interfering in the other immortal gods' plans. Realize that this has never happened before. The gods have always worked as one, but your father disliked their cruel mischief. You see, Glantis, he sacrificed his power and freedom for all of Brendonia." Golis stated the last sentence with the most respectful voice.

"Why don't these immortals just destroy me?" Glantis questioned, thinking of what he might do.

"This, fortunately for us, they cannot do. You see, then, they too would be guilty of the same crime," Golis said with a flare in his voice. "Paradoxically, we have the immortals at a disadvantage."

Glantis stood staring into the sky. "What of my mother?"

"She died during your birth, Glantis. She was very beautiful in mind, spirit, and body. She is buried in a graveyard in the village of Celesta. Her name was Ashlena. Her grave is the only unknown in the cemetery."

"Ashlena," Glantis expressed aloud, trying to remember, although he knew it was impossible. He looked around the valley admiring its beauty. "So green," he said taking a deep breath.

"Yes, before you were born, all of Brendonia looked like this. Slowly, it began to deteriorate since the continent divided, for reasons unclear to me."

"And it will once again," Trefmore stated boldly.

"I have been here many centuries, Glantis. As it seems, you are special. A god created you as a key to change the fate of our world, brought here to set the path straight so that all the races of Brendonia can live in peace again. You may not know it, but I am a race. I am the everlasting of my race, not like that of your father's immortality, but of nature's spirit world. My roots once ran under the whole continent. The other trees you see out of this valley are my eyes. Sadly, when the continent split, my roots were severed. I can no longer see anything on the upper continent. Only lower Brendonia and parts of the Eastland remain visible."

"Do you know what broke the other continents apart?"

"Yes, Glantis, I saw it for only a brief second. A powerful druid has risen to power among the druid cults of upper Brendonia. It was that druid and his disciples that cracked and sunk the hardened earth. It was six druids. They call themselves the Council of Sinx. Judging from what I picked up in their thoughts, they seem to want to cut off lower Brendonia's water supply. All my trees above the Kantar Mountains have been dying more and more over the years, cut off from the freshwaters of Lake Infinity. The only source of water for my children is the Jade River. As you know, the Jade's waters are the life's blood of lower Brendonia, and without its nourishment, all the forests and animals will last no more than a few weeks. My fear is that the Jade is the next target on the evil highmaster druid's list. I have seen trouble along the Jade. My eyes have become misty in certain areas in the last few days. I fear the druids are up to something. As of now, all the trees of lower Brendonia are surviving, yet only because of that single river.

"Who is the master druid?" Glantis asked.

"The druid's name is Bernac, and I am afraid he has fixed it so the continent can never be restored again. Times have changed for good, Glantis."

"Then how can I restore the trees and stop a war from happening?" Glantis asked in a worried tone.

"There is one other thing that can save our trees: rain. As you know, we have had a drought all year. The Jade River is the lifeline of lower Brendonia's trees, yet even the river cannot replace the rains forever. The time is now, Glantis. Bernac is thirsty for power. I fear the Jade River is his next target. As I've told you, my sight in certain areas along the river has faded. Something is awry."

"What of the rain?" Glantis questioned quickly.

"Only Bernac can restore that. His magic holds the rain from falling on lower Brendonia. The solution is either to persuade him to remove the spell or to kill him, neither of which is an easy task. Bernac must be getting stronger. Otherwise, he would have stopped the rain fifteen years ago. Fortunately, for us, he didn't have the power. If he had, survival would have been impossible."

Golis' thoughts slowly drained from Glantis' mind. Glantis began to have doubts. It seemed the fate of the world rested on his shoulders. "How can I be expected to...?" It was at this point that Glantis lost control of his mind. Suddenly, his inner mind strengthened, driven by a new force. His doubts became virtually nonexistent. His godlike powers were taking temporary control over him.

"I will find this Bernac, great one, and if possible, restore this continent's water."

"Do what you must. As long as this valley and the trees around me still exist, my race will survive."

"Goodbye, Golis, I shall not fail you. I shall not fail my mother and father."

"Glantis Trefmore. Remember. Bernac knows nothing of you. This may be something you can use against him. Most important, don't let your human side take over your thoughts. There is no room for emotion in what you must do. Bernac has much in common with you, Glantis. Don't let him turn your human thoughts to his bidding. Be careful..." was the last thought that burst into his head as he passed through the black wall into the Elven Forest.

When Glantis returned to the camp, it was night. He found Drek sitting before a blazing fire while Oonic sat next to him chewing on a piece of dried meat. Glantis walked through the brush into the clearing toward the fire.

"I assume you found the valley?" Drek asked throwing another log into the fire.

"Yes, and I talked to Golis for what seemed to be hours."

Drek smiled. "You were gone quite a long time. Did you have trouble finding it?"

Glantis shuffled over to the fire and nodded yes.

That night, Glantis retold all the things Golis had said to him. Drek seemed shocked at the news. Although it did explain the bizarreness of the man in black named Pantos,

Drek's only recollection of him was of his dreamlike aura and his demanding instructions. Many times did he try to sort out what happened on that mysterious night over fifteen years ago. Drek ended up snuffing out his thoughts as well as the fire, for Glantis was very tired from his trip to the valley and had fallen asleep.

Drek then got up and silently walked into the forest. A great many nights of the mage's life were devoted to the payment of the debt for his reprocessed soul. What he did on those nights no one knew but him.

When Glantis awoke, he found it was close to noon. He saw Drek packing up all their things upon Plolate's broad back. The great ocherous sat unmoving, except for its eyes seemingly scanning the forest. Next, Oonic started growling ferociously into the forest. Glantis stood up while grabbing his silver axe. The sounds of hoof beats resonated through the forest. The increasing loudness told them the horseman was traveling directly at them. Within moments, the horse came crashing through the brush. Instantly, the horseman began to pull forcefully on the reins. The huge horse lifted its front hooves off the ground, whinnying loudly. Glantis raised his axe. "Who are you?" he said. Taking a second look he continued, "What are you?"

"Pardon," Drek said. "He has not seen many elven folk."

"I am Parlock. Who are you?" The elven man looked at them with suspicion.

Glantis answered without any hint of hesitation. "I am Glantis Trefmore, advisor to King Hestin and beside me is my foster father, Drek Trefmore."

"If he is your foster father, why do you use his name?" the elf asked, still wary.

"I bear his name out of the respect and love I have for him. He is the only father I've ever known."

The elf's mouth dropped open. It took Glantis and Drek a moment to determine what the problem was until they remembered Plolate. The elven man stared in disbelief at the giant ocherous. The beast was sitting so still that he had not seen it.

"How is it you travel with an ocherous?" Parlock asked astonished. "Who are you men?" the elf asked again, forgetting his previous questions.

This time Drek answered in an impatient tone. "I am Drek, and this is Glantis Trefmore," the mage rasped, his seething voice grasping Parlock's attention.

"Well, Glantis, I see you wear Brendonia's crest. I should tell you, the king is summoning all his soldiers to return to the castle," the elf told them, still staring at Plolate.

"Why?" Glantis questioned in a worried tone.

"Haven't you heard? The Jade River has ceased to flow with water. It is now almost completely dry."

"I only left a day ago," Glantis said, not believing the elf's words.

"Come then," Parlock spoke. "My lord will wish to see you to draw up a plan of action."

Drek and Glantis looked at each other questionably, and then quickly mounted Plolate. The elf trotted westward toward the elven kingdom.

"Up, Plolate, and do not lose the elf," Drek called out.

Plolate spread his great wings, quickly ascending. Even in the sky, Glantis could not find the horseman, yet Plolate seemed to follow the elf with ease.

"It's the elven magic. It makes it almost impossible for normal men to see through the thick brush," Drek explained.

For the duration of the flight, Glantis struggled with his disbelief that the Jade River had run dry. Golis' deepest fear was true. The Jade River had been the druids' next target. This brought Glantis to a new revelation. If Golis was right about the river, then he was telling the truth about his parents, one being a god and the other a human. He was, indeed, a demigod.

"How?" Glantis thought. "Why me? How did I get into this mess? I should have refused the forest master and told him to save the land himself or to get someone else. Why had I accepted? Why did I vow to kill Bernac?" Glantis shook his head. He could not have said that. Yet he knew it. Glantis ducked his head while taking a deep breath trying to calm down. His boyish fears were resurfacing.

In what seemed much less than an hour, they began to descend again.

"How can we land there, Drek?" Glantis asked while looking down at the abundance of trees beneath them.

"Watch," Drek pointed downward. Just before they would seemingly crash into the treetops, the trees disappeared, and before Glantis could tell what happened, Plolate had landed. Glantis looked around and, once again, knew it was magic that hid the beautiful elven city. Glantis quickly dismounted Plolate with a leap. He was astonished at the softness of the moist ground. Glantis looked around in amazement at all the beautiful wooden houses. Everywhere he looked, he saw wood. It was breathtaking the way the elves blended the beautiful buildings with the surrounding trees.

"They are truly experts with the shaping and construction of wood." Drek walked up from behind with Oonic right beside him.

There was no sign of Parlock or any other elf. Although, as they looked closer, they saw that many eyes watched from the safety of their homes.

"No doubt they have never seen the likes of us before," Glantis stated.

"Yes," Drek said with a short sigh. "Although the king meets with them on occasion, I'm afraid it is not on a social basis. During the Boundary Wars, all the people of both elven and human races knew what the other looked like, but that was many generations ago. Perhaps Plolate landing in their village without warning might have something to do with it." Drek smiled at Glantis.

Finally, Parlock returned with several servants following him. Parlock met them with a smile. "Welcome to Torka. These men will take you to your quarters where you can bathe and rest after which you are invited for dinner at that building." Parlock pointed to a large, wooden structure. It stood in the middle of the city. Two beautiful trees stood on each side of the building. The branches of the trees seemingly wrapped their caring arms around the building's rooftop. Small plants and flowers decorated the light brown wood of the building. Glantis regretfully turned away from the wondrous sight, following the elven servant. They walked past many small homes. Each decorated differently, as if each house represented the family living within. Some homes hid under an abundance of grape vines, while others were decorated with small plants and flowers. Glantis gasped at all the different plants. He had never seen so many species before.

"I see you're taking interest in the village," the servant said. "Each house you see along this path attracts different plants. The family living there attracts different plant growth by means of the elves' own individuality and essence. You might better understand it as similar to what you call magic. I do not expect you to understand, though, but it is our way."

Glantis just smiled at the slim-looking elf and followed him into a small house. The elf was wrong. He did understand, all too well.

"Bathe and rest. Do you wish me to return and wake you before dinner?" the elf asked.

"Yes, thank you." Glantis looked up with a smile.

The servant nodded, and then swiftly left the room.

Glantis quickly bathed, after which he tried one of the beds in the room. The bed was very firm, yet comfortable. He rested on his back thinking of the elves. It seemed strange the way their wet-looking skin reflected light. When he saw the servant outside, he had a pale green look. Once inside, however, his skin had turned dark as if it was reflecting the light around it. Glantis was impressed with the elven village of Torka. It seemed like such a wonderful place to live, a tranquil village with the most beautiful surroundings of plant life. It would be a shame for such a village to perish. Hidden or not, the evil would spread and eventually destroy Torka as well. Glantis thought about all the things he learned these past few days, and he easily fell asleep.

The servant returned within an hour. The elf set down Glantis' clothes and axe on a table near the bed. "I took the liberty of washing your clothes and restoring your axe. I hope you do not mind."

"Thank you," Glantis replied groggily, not really hearing what the elf had said.

"The dinner will begin soon, so I suggest you get dressed and go to the hall," the servant finished, opening the door, "oh, and don't forget your weapon." The elf smiled wryly, closing the door behind him.

"Good try, my friend," Glantis said to himself. "I may not know much about the elves, but that custom, I know. It was simple, really," Glantis told himself. "All you do is wait to be addressed and stand before the elf lord with a show of arms. Then offer your weapon to him, a simple way to show respect among the elven army. It is obvious some of the elves are not too comfortable with humans in their village."

Glantis finished dressing himself and reached down picking up his silver axe. His eyes opened wide with amazement. The polished silver and wooden handle looked as if its life had been restored, carved only moments ago. Glantis, very pleased with his weapon, began to swing it around. Then realizing the idea of being late, he quickly dressed and left the house walking swiftly toward the hall. He walked on a path that led directly to the building. Outside, not one elf walked the streets. Glantis could still feel, however, the eyes upon him from inside the houses. When he reached the hall, he climbed three steps to the entrance. Two guards stood on either side of giant double doors that were already open. He walked into a short hallway. Loudly, the doors closed behind him.

"I must be the last one in," he thought to himself. Glantis quickly walked toward the light, turning right then left into a giant room filled with torchlight. Paintings and tapestries covered the walls. In the center of the room was a sturdy, wooden table with legs shaped like the trunk of a tree. Around the table sat Drek, Parlock, and whom he imagined must be the elf lord. Only one seat remained vacant. Glantis slowly walked over to it. Before sitting, he held out the handle of his axe to the elf lord.

"There is no need for that here," the elf lord said waving his hand.

"Eat and then I will explain," the elf lord spoke dimly. All the food was already on the table. There was not a server nor another person in the room. The meal was quiet and very fast.

When the elf lord saw everyone was finished, he stood up and began to walk around the table, the sound of his heavy boots clunking on the floor.

"All of you in this room may call me Grengale," the elf lord said. "What we speak of now will only be told to the King of Brendonia." There was a moment of silence. "I received a message today from the king himself. It stated that someone had dammed our water supply. Now we all know that when the center of the Brendonian continent sank, the freshwaters of Lake Infinity no longer fed the trees to the east and west of lower Brendonia's Kantar Mountains in time of drought. Now everything west of the mountains is slowly dying, struggling to feed off the Jade River. Our present survival is dependent upon the freshwater spring that runs beneath the Kantar Mountains. This spring is the lifeline of all the things east of the mountains. Well, my friends, that line has been cut off. The Jade River has ceased to flow across the continent with its cooling waters. It now appears as a dry ditch!" Grengale pounded his hand down onto the table. "Only the rain can buy us more time, but I remind you it has neither snowed nor rained this season. It is to my knowledge that the druids of upper Brendonia are the cause of our problems."

"How do you know it is the druids that hold our fate?" Drek asked in a cutting whisper.

"My scouts have seen small bands of druids on the west side of the Kantar Mountains in the Bolonwood Forest. We know now that they have dammed the Jade River. My guess is that they are trying to starve the land and us. If successful, they could easily take over our kingdom. Once all the trees are gone, it will not be difficult to find our secret village.

"What do you plan to do, Grengale?" Glantis asked.

Grengale quickly answered, "We must immediately send word to King Hestin, confirming that it is definitely the druids who dammed the river. We must receive the king's consent to attack the druids' camp and reopen the Jade."

"Where is the river being closed off?" Glantis questioned.

Parlock then spoke out. "It will not be easy to flush the druids out. Although most of them are druid bardes and are not heavily armed, they are large in numbers and dug in quite deeply. My guess is we will have to force our way into the caverns, killing every one of them until we reach the blockage. They have probably dammed the river at its source. How, I have no idea. The source is a freshwater spring located deep beneath the Kantar Mountains."

"Then how do we get there?" Glantis asked, not understanding.

This time Grengale answered, "There is a series of caves leading under the mountains to the spring. Bardes are spreading all over the Bolonwood Forest, especially near a well-known cave entrance that leads under the Kantars. One thing I do not understand is where they are putting the water." Grengale paused thinking of his question. "Eventually the water would have to overflow."

No one answered.

Grengale put his thoughts behind him. "Tomorrow at dawn, Parlock will ride with you to the castle as fast as possible.

Glantis blurted out, "On Plolate, we could fly to the castle now and get there by daybreak." Drek looked at Grengale and nodded in agreement.

"So be it." Grengale rose. He called his servants to enter. Before anyone left the hall, Grengale spoke softly. "Quickly, my friends, we haven't much time."

Glantis felt strange knowing that a war would soon start in Brendonia. He felt even stranger that he was one of the first ones to know about it.

Within a few minutes, Glantis, Drek, and Parlock began to climb onto Plolate. Oonic dashed out from the woods and jumped aboard. Plolate began to flap his great wings ascending into the air. Glantis looked up seeing the dark sky with only a few stars out. Once they reached a certain height, it began to get colder. Drek pointed down showing Glantis that the illusion over the elven village had returned. Glantis shook his head in amazement as he looked directly below Plolate, only to see the forest trees.

Plolate flew fast. Within moments, the Elven Forest was beyond them. The night was bitter and cold. The travelers drew their cloaks around them trying to warm themselves. Glantis looked ahead, seeing small traces of the Jade River's delta. For now, it contained some water, but in a few days, it would evaporate from the sun's heat.

"Just beyond the delta is my home and the village of Celesta," Glantis thought. How he missed those places of comfort and warmth. He laughed remembering what he considered a catastrophe at home. Nothing, nothing compared to the hardships that were arising.

Those days were over. Glantis was being forced to change from boy to man overnight. As much as he wanted to go home and relax, he knew he could not. Great sacrifices were made to create him, and he would not let his mother and father down. Time was running out for Brendonia, and he knew he was somehow the key to stop the clock.

CHAPTER 4
STRANGE WATERS

KING HESTIN AWOKE EARLY from his warm bed to the sound of the alarms. He heard doors opening and closing throughout the castle. From what his advisor told him, an ocherous had been sighted flying toward the castle.

"Probably too much ale to drink," the king thought with agitation. He quickly got dressed; there was no use in trying to go back to sleep. Whatever the guard saw might be vital to the kingdom's safety. The king scowled at all the things happening in Brendonia.

A solid knocking sounded on his door.

"What is it now?" the king grunted, straining to pull up his pants as the door opened.

Surlonthes and Levantia stood in the doorway not daring to laugh at the king's awkward positioning.

"Father," Prince Surlonthes addressed informally, "there really *is* an ocherous flying toward the castle, and it carries passengers."

"Passengers? On an ocherous? I thought those birds were practically extinct?"

"Apparently not, Sire," Levantia answered the king. The king, tired of being in the dark about everything, pushed his way out the door with Surlonthes and Levantia following behind.

Plolate screeched a frightening note, waking up its riders. Drek helped by shaking Glantis and Parlock, informing them that the castle was just ahead. Plolate glided onto the causeway road in front of the castle's iron doors. Its feet touched the dirt as its wings beat to a stop, kicking up a thin wall of dust.

Glantis was the first to leave Plolate's feathery back. He held up his right hand and yelled to the high walls of the castle. "Sire, it is I, Glantis. I bring an elf as well as news of the druids!"

The king answered by signaling to open the iron doors. Guards quickly scrambled to the mechanism that released the iron bolt. With a sharp snap, the lock clicked and the doors began to swing open.

Drek slipped off Plolate, followed by Parlock. The three men removed their packs from Plolate's deep feathers. Oonic was already off the ocherous running around wildly.

Just now did the new morning sun begin to peek over the horizon. From the castle, it was an awesome sight. Not far below the castle walls stood a beast not seen in Brendonia for over thirty years, its deep orange color still well remembered by those lucky enough and old enough to have seen it once before. The king was rather stunned. The bird brought back memories of when he was a boy, horrible times of war and aerial combat. He saw hundreds of the creatures covering the blue skies fighting back massive dragons and everything else that threatened their existence. The Boundary Wars were ruthless battles in which all the races lost. Total chaos had spread across the kingdom, and the possibility of peace had seemed far off. King Hestin breathed a sigh of relief. It could never be that bad again. Or could it?

The weary travelers stalked into the castle. The guards greeted them once they entered the courtyard. Glantis looked around; the castle was somehow different. There were fully armed guards all along the walls. To the left, beautiful, top-grade stallions filled the stables. The armory was packed with sparkling chainmail alongside hundreds of shiny swords straight from the forge.

Levantia and Surlonthes strode toward Glantis and his group. In between them was King Hestin, his golden crown sparkling in the dawn's new light.

"Your majesty," Drek bowed along with everyone. "I am Drek Trefmore, Glantis' foster father and caretaker. This is Parlock, whom you already know, from the elven village of Torka. We intercepted him returning to his home in the Elven Forest."

The king nodded in recognition, shaking the hands of the two. "It is a shame we are meeting under such conditions, Parlock. May I say that you are an excellent messenger," the king complimented.

The elf nodded in silent thanks, his translucent skin reflecting the morning sky.

"Sire," Glantis said. "Could we please get some food for the animals?"

"I have already taken care of that. Look." Surlonthes pointed to the old road.

They all looked, seeing the pyren chewing something while Plolate snapped its beak on a heaping piece of meat.

The king watched in awe at the strength of the ocherous.

"He is the last of his kind," Drek whispered, almost reading the king's mind.

The king stared, his eyes beginning to moisten. Then he spoke out softly to all of them. "I had no idea they were struggling without water, too. I was only thinking of my people. These animals are all part of my kingdom, and I abandoned them. After that great bird passes on, we will never see another of its kind. I can only imagine how the other animals have suffered." The king paused, his face wet with tears. Then, his face began to harden. He looked to the horizon. "The druids will pay for this. They have almost succeeded in destroying the kingdom by stealing our water and stopping our rain. Now they have dammed the Jade River. We cannot ignore these signs, or second-guess the culprit. The druids are the cause and we are going to retaliate by launching an attack on them."

Drek and Glantis showed no emotion while the others were sad. Glantis stared into nothingness. Perhaps he saw what the king saw.

"Let us go to my private quarters and devise a plan," the king said in a bold voice. "We have stood here too long. What the druids have done is unforgivable. Those vermin have planned this for years. They have been waiting patiently. For fifteen years we have been cut from communication with them, and in that time they have been devising ways to successfully destroy us." The king led them to the inner city. Silence dominated as they walked through the castle. Soldiers and common folk rushed around the castle preparing for the worst. Suddenly, as if coming out of a trance, the king turned to Parlock. "Do the druids know we are aware of them?"

"No," Parlock answered. "As soon as our watchmen spotted them, we sent that elf to you. He then relayed your message to me about the Jade stopping, and I took it to my lord."

"Yes, I received that messenger two days ago," the king remembered. "If the druids think they're still a secret, we'll have an edge."

King Hestin motioned to some nearby servants. "Get these men food. Then bring them to the counseling room within an hour."

Glantis and the others had finished eating and were now in the king's counseling chamber discussing the druids. They sat at a heavy, wooden table surrounded by thirty or more chairs. Many colorful tapestries hung on the walls around them.

The door opened revealing King Hestin. Behind the king was Clifford Janestin, the strategic commander for the armies.

"I trust everyone has eaten well?" King Hestin asked. They all nodded in agreement. The king continued, "For those of you who do not know this man, he is Clifford Janestin. He is my top strategic officer." Everyone acknowledged Janestin by nodding.

Janestin and the king sat down. The strategic officer pulled out a map and laid it square on the table.

"We know the druids are somewhere along the Kantar Mountains, here," he pointed to the map. "They obviously came by way of the New Sea. According to their location, they must have traveled through the ocherous nesting trees to the Bolonwood Forest. From there, they found an entrance to the caverns, located the spring, and dammed it," Janestin concluded looking up from the map.

Glantis spoke out, "Why is it that the only thing the druids are doing is damming our water? Sooner or later they knew we would check out the mountains."

"That's what bothers me," Janestin stated. "I have taken troops to scout the Bimbalian Forest as far as the lower Kantar Mountains, but there is no sign of druids."

"They're foolish if they think they can withstand my army by damming our water," Hestin announced.

"I agree, father, but we know they are not stupid. Besides, they might be the ones responsible for breaking the continent," Surlonthes reminded his father.

At this point, Glantis shifted in his chair. Drek gave him a look, and he knew immediately to say nothing of the druids' destruction of the continent. Besides, what purpose would it serve? If anything, all it would do is discourage the army. An army that fights an enemy that has the power to disintegrate hardened earth is not much of an army.

"He's right, my lord," Janestin intervened. "Another problem we should be concerned with is their fighting tactics. Let's not forget about the magic they perform which we know nothing about."

"But remember," Drek cut in, gaining the group's full attention, "during the Boundary Wars, only the highest in the order, known as druids, had the strongest magic, while the vates had only the ability to perform dangerous spells. The bardes couldn't perform magic at all, and they now make up almost the whole population," Drek finished, staring at the members.

"Yes, but what of their strategy?" Parlock questioned. "For all we know, they could have another encampment somewhere."

"Highly unlikely, at least not on the continent. We send out daily checks throughout the kingdom. If an attack on the kingdom is possible, it will have to come by sea," Janestin explained.

"Meaning no disrespect, Sire, but what do you intend to do? At this moment, the whole Elven kingdom is on standby," Parlock reminded him.

The king spoke. "For the first time, yesterday, I received a letter carried by a brave dwarf from the far city of Lore. One of our ships picked him up along lower Brendonia's north shoreline in a small boat. The dwarf died from lack of food and water. In his left hand, he held this note." King Hestin pulled it from his tunic and began to read:

"Lord Hestin, this has to be the hundredth letter we've sent to you. The druids have obviously been intercepting our carriers. The Druid Order has enslaved many of our people, men, women, and children. We are defenseless, and I fear they will get to you next. The druids have come under a new power, the Druid Lord Bernac, the last of the full-blooded druidic magic. Beware of his power, my friend, for he and his disciples are strong. Help us Edward, but remember, as you know yourself, I have a heart of stone within me."

Gullon

The group was silent. The king folded up the note, care-fully placing it into his tunic. "All hope is not lost, my friends. If I know Gullon, that last sentence means he is attempting to gather an army." Silence dominated the room as they waited for the king to explain.

King Hestin then went on to answer the elf's previous question. "Janestin and a group of 1,000 troops will ride out at tomorrow's first light toward the elven village of Torka. There they will seek the elf lord, Grengale, and inform him of the current happenings. The elves will surely send some of their men out to help Janestin." The king paused, thinking. "The troops will then attack the entrance where the druids stand. My hope is that they will break through the caverns and successfully regain control of the Jade River. If things get hot, I have directed Janestin to retreat to the elven city, regroup, and immediately send for more forces from the castle. Our problem is we cannot risk leaving the castle unprotected until we are sure there is only one encampment. It's possible that's what the druids are trying to do. If they took the castle with no resistance, we would need an army twenty times the strength of our own to retake Castle Brendonia," the king finished, looking at Janestin to take over.

Janestin quickly followed up on the king's words. "It is possible my troops and I will not be able to penetrate the druid forces. We have no way of knowing how many men they have buried in those caverns. This is where your group comes in." Janestin looked directly at Levantia. "Levantia,

Surlonthes, and Glantis are to follow the Jade River to its end at the mountains. There should be some hole leading directly down into the caverns below the mountains."

"Kind of like going in the back door," Levantia presumed.

"Exactly," Janestin answered. "If we fail, it might be possible for your force to reopen the blockage and escape.

"And what if they do open the river, they'll be smashed against the cavern walls by the water," Drek reminded Janestin.

"According to the dwarves, there are several higher ledges to climb up, safe from the swift-flowing waters. If you wait on these ledges for a short period, the water will begin to slow, refilling the Jade deltas," Janestin explained. "Here, I have an old dwarven map of the caverns beneath the Kantar Mountains. It is rather old, but the caverns are almost unchanging and should be the same since the first dwarven explorations."

Drek and Parlock silently discussed the situation. When finished, Drek raised his head and addressed the king. "Parlock and I have decided to go with Levantia, if your majesty will allow it."

The king paused in thought.

Noticing the king's hesitation, Drek spoke out again. "Who knows what beasts live down in those waters and caves. I am afraid it will take quite a bit more than swords and arrows to fight the things roaming below the mountains. And, I am the only one here that can work magic."

The king looked up staring at the mysterious man. He was not surprised that Drek was a master of the ancient arts. King Hestin broke out of his thoughts. "It is done. I grant you your request. Janestin will leave tomorrow at first light. Levantia's group will leave in two days' time. This should give Janestin the time he needs to travel the extra distance. On the third day, come morning, Janestin will attack the druid encampment, causing uproar and confusion. I hope Levantia's group will be in place at that time. They won't be expecting you from behind, so you will probably be able to somehow unblock the river. Let me remind you that if this plan fails, our water supply will be depleted in one month's time. My people cannot live, let alone fight, without water. The land has already begun to wilt and with the Jade presently gone, in a month's time the land will be severely damaged beyond repair. All the trees and grasslands will begin to brown beyond revival. We have left the Jade deltas for the animals. The water there will last another five to six days in this heat. It has already become stagnant and will soon be completely dried up."

It was noon when the council finished. They all went to rest in their assigned rooms, skipping lunch for rationing purposes. Later that evening, the small group had a private dinner with the king who insisted on a meal free of any talk of druids or strategies. They ate in silence.

Glantis stood on the fairway in front of Castle Brendonia, saddling his horse. He kneeled down and pulled the strap tightly around the stallion's belly. He quickly scooped up his pack and laid it upon the horse's broad back. It had been a day since Clifford Janestin and a group of 1,000 soldiers rode off toward the elven city of Torka. According to the plan, Janestin should be arriving there sometime today. If so, they were now preparing for the attack at tomorrow's first light. This gave Levantia's group one full day to reach the cavern and find the river's blockage.

Glantis secured his pack containing provisions and his mighty battle-axe. He looked up seeing Levantia and Surlonthes riding toward him. Glantis grinned seeing the two together. Surlonthes was like a brother to him, and he was glad to see the prince was attracting her. Over these many days, Glantis realized he would not be able to have a relationship such as theirs. He was beginning to understand the reason for his birth in the land: to save it from destruction and from the unruly order of evil that wished so eagerly to take it over.

Glantis wondered what he would do if these things ended. Could he live a normal life if he succeeded?

"Ready, Glantis?" Levantia said with a smile. Glantis answered by mounting his horse and riding to meet them. Shortly, Drek and Parlock rode up alongside them ready for departure.

Suddenly, Oonic's bark attracted the group's attention. Oonic stood near Plolate who was lying with his neck and head comfortably on the ground. It seemed strange to Glantis that Plolate was relaxed while Oonic sat up panting, begging to come along. Glantis dismounted his horse and walked over to the eager pyren. He kneeled down and softly explained to Oonic that it was safer for him at the castle. The pyren understood and began to whimper, lying down and dropping his head to rest on his front legs. Oonic wanted to help, but would never disobey his master. Unknown to Glantis, Oonic knew by fate that he would once again help the lovable boy. The mysterious god, Pantos, had told Oonic, just before sending him on his journey, that he would save the warrior three times: once as a boy, once as a man, and once as a god. Only after Oonic fulfilled his destiny would he be able to return to his own kind.

Glantis petted Oonic, hoping this would not be the last time he would see the brave pyren. After bidding Oonic and Plolate farewell, Glantis returned to his horse.

Parlock then spoke out in a soothing tone, "They understand."

Glantis nodded, looking back at the castle and animals. He somehow felt he would return safely. His last thought was whether it would ever be as it was when growing up in the Wood of Kinet.

"Ride," Levantia commanded, her voice echoing through the brightening sky. The five rode off across the Brendonian Plains, heading toward the Bimbalian Forest and the Jade River.

King Hestin and his advisor watched them leave from high upon the king's favorite tower. The five horses slowly transformed into barely visible specks on the vast canvas of the Brendonian Plains.

"What do you think their chances are of unblocking the river?" the king curiously asked his advisor.

"It will take quite a miracle, Sire," the advisor spoke his feelings.

"Indeed," the king responded, watching the riders, especially his son, disappear into the distance.

They rode about three hours before they reached the well-known bend in the Jade, once filled with refreshing, rushing water, now just a deep crevice of mud. The companions dismounted their horses and took some food and water from their saddle packs.

"Drink little and give the horses only a mouthful. We still have a few hours of travel," Drek warned. The party rested for fifteen minutes and then rode off again. In some areas, the brush was too thick for the horses, forcing them to take many time-consuming detours. Mostly, the group followed the Jade River, riding along its bare banks. They followed the river for several hours until they finally reached the Kantar Mountains. Tons of hard, gray rock blocked their way. The only passage between was a breach where the river dried up.

"We will have to walk the horses in the river's ditch. The end of this passage should lead us straight to the river's exit," Surlonthes suggested.

Surlonthes quickly took the lead, ignoring the penetrating stare of Levantia, who was supposedly leading this expedition. The others slowly followed, sinking deeper in the mud with each step forward. Glantis and Surlonthes had the least trouble, being the tallest; however, Drek never complained. Once through the narrow passage, they quickly climbed out of the ditch onto the riverbank. The horses were still whinnying, scared of being trapped. Everyone was covered with mud up to mid-thigh, except Drek, who had not a trace of mud on his flowing, black robes. The others, however, did not seem to notice.

They walked their horses along the rocky riverside, looking for an entrance under the mountains.

"Look, up ahead," Glantis pointed, discovering a cave-like structure. The cave could only be entered from a muddy ditch. Glantis ran up ahead almost dragging his horse along through the mud. "Don't worry," he yelled back smiling. "The entrance has a rocky floor."

Relieved that they would not be traveling in mud, the others began to gather at the entrance. They all dismounted and secured the packs for travel by foot.

Drek looked at Glantis with a half-smile, pointing at the small pool of water near the base of the entrance. "The horses will be fine, Glantis."

In moments, everyone was ready. Levantia was the first to enter the dark cave. Cautiously, the others followed her into the cavern.

Clifford Janestin and his troops arrived at Torka around midday. The elves had recognized the king's standard and had ridden out to meet them. From there, they guided them safely through the beautiful Elven Forest to Torka.

Now, Janestin walked with Grengale, the elf lord. The two were walking around seeing to the village's progress. Grengale had ordered his men to restring all the bows and to forge an abundance of arrowheads. The elven women readied the horses by covering them with green, multicolored battle coats. Janestin did not like this and wanted to keep the king's colorful coats upon the horses. Grengale, who said the camouflage coats would make them harder to see by the druids, later convinced Janestin to forgo the brightly colored coats.

Meanwhile, Janestin's men sat sharpening their swords and daggers for the fight. Some of his archers worked with the elves, learning how to construct better bows and arrows. When it came to wood, the elves looked as though they were the ones responsible for creating it. Elves constructed amazing things out of wood.

Janestin and Grengale called a meeting before nightfall. There were now over 2,000 men. According to what Grengale's scouts reported, it was an amount sufficient to take the caverns and unblock the river.

"Fellow soldiers," Janestin called out. The men were all huddled around several small fires in the village square. "Tomorrow at dawn we will ride in four formations, each relatively equal in size. We will travel through the Bolonwood Forest along the Kantar Mountains until we reach the druids' camp. Elven scouts claim the druids have spread themselves in front of the cave's entrance. The plan is to force our way into the cave, pushing the druids back into the entrance to a dead end and fighting them until they give up. The next step is to find the location of the dam and destroy it. If, at any time we're losing, or there are too many druids, retreat on my orders back here for reinforcements. Any questions?"

The orders were straightforward. The men mumbled in a quiet understanding and slowly began to disperse to their tents or homes.

Janestin turned to Grengale. "It doesn't look good, Grengale. The men are not excited for battle. They must be worried about the druids' magic. We must remember it has been fifteen years since the continent's division. None of us really know what we're in for," Janestin concluded.

"Yes, and they're the only ones capable of sinking the center of Brendonia," Grengale broke in. "Their magic must be twice the strength by now. The only way the kingdom dealt with them before was by sheer numbers," Grengale stopped with a short sigh.

Janestin replied, "I know what you mean, but if we can get our water back it shouldn't be too hard to stop the war before it starts." The two men looked at each other, hoping. Deep in their hearts, they both knew this was just the beginning.

Drek guessed it was now night. They had neither seen nor heard any sign of druids in the cave. The cavern was knee-deep in unmoving water. The floors and sides were lined with sharp rock and treacherous walkways. The further they went into the cave the darker it became. After a moment, each of them pulled out a torch. Drek told them to hold the torches straight out in front of themselves. The party did as he said. Drek's eyes glowed light orange, then, in a spark of light, all five torches lit up. The members smiled at the amazing magic.

"You best get used to seeing magic," Drek spoke in hushed tones. "It is the druids' way."

The members comprehended and pushed on through the caverns. Levantia was leading, followed by Glantis, who splashed through the water. Then came Surlonthes, holding his giant broadsword upright. Behind Surlonthes was Parlock, carrying his bow with an arrow notched in anticipation. In the rear walked Drek, holding his torch high, staring deeply into the darkness. Occasionally, he would fall back making sure no one followed.

The travelers waded throughout the caverns for hours. It seemed like they had not made any progress since they first entered. Drek had lit their torches more than once during the journey. They were running low on torches, and they had to start conserving supplies, using only one for light. They stopped to eat earlier, yet despite the little time that passed, they were getting hungry again. In the dark caverns, the judgment of time became unknown.

"Stop," Levantia said, holding her hand out behind her.

The weary travelers listened, hearing the sound of splashing water.

"There must be running water up ahead, the spring," Levantia spoke out.

The group slowly walked through the water toward the sound. They reached an end to the tunnel. It opened up into a large inner lake. Despite the bad lighting, they could see the ceiling was much higher, extending up fifty feet or more. The water was not very deep along the sides. Glantis swam a little ways out and found a steep drop off toward the center. He swiftly swam back wanting to leave the cold water.

"It looks like this inner lake was drained below the entrance. Then the water ceased at the castle. This very lake is probably somewhere close to the actual freshwater spring." Glantis concluded, "This can't be the spring because there's not much movement in this water."

They all began to spread apart searching the walls for other passageways. Levantia and Parlock waded to the right, scanning the walls with torches. Drek remained at the doorway, while Glantis and Surlonthes went left. The water was swirling in many directions. Glantis scratched his head, wondering how they had heard the quiet splashing of the waves brushing up against the cavern walls from such a distance. Glantis also could not understand why the cavern walls were wet.

A huge splash in the middle of the lake answered his thoughts. Water flew everywhere making the party close their eyes.

"Get out of the water!" Surlonthes yelled in a rumbling voice, his eyes still closed. His command barely sounded over the splashing.

A large snake-like beast rose out of the water almost as high as the ceiling. The serpent's screech caused a cacophonic echo so horrifying it forced them to cover their ears. Glantis and Surlonthes had already left the water, heading toward the entrance. Surlonthes was busy distracting the monster, swinging his broadsword wildly. Glantis dropped his pack to the ground and pulled out his mighty axe.

Levantia and Parlock had weapons out, but they were cut off from the entrance. The beast screeched at the two and began to hiss fiendishly. It had them trapped. Parlock immediately shot off two arrows from his bow. Both struck the serpent squarely in its neck. The slimy beast turned around lashing its tail out, sending both Parlock and Levantia flying onto the rocky shoreline. The serpent ducked underwater, disappearing from sight. The waters gradually became calm.

All too soon, the water once again began to swirl. The monster rose up again, this time closer to the entrance. The beast sent huge waves of rolling water, causing Surlonthes and Glantis to slip. Raising his hands, Drek launched a burst of flame toward the serpent. The beast screeched in fright, but the fireball overshot it. Again, the serpent swung its tail, this time sending large amounts of water directly at Drek. The water swallowed the mage, throwing him back into the cavern's entranceway.

In all the confusion, Glantis had dropped his axe. The large waves had thrown him up against the wall, and the impact caused him to drop his weapon. Glantis began searching for the battle-axe. His friends were nowhere in sight. His hands combed the lake's rocky floor. The savage beast was slithering toward him. At that very moment, Glantis' hands wrapped around the familiar axe handle. The beast snapped its jaws. In a timeless motion, Glantis pulled the axe out of the water while diving to safety. Missing its prey, the serpent jerked backwards. Glantis landed in the shallow water to his left, his hips smashing hard against the jagged rocks beneath the lake's surface. At that moment, a strange rage overtook Glantis. His eyes began to glow blue. The serpent was setting up for a second attack. This time it would not miss.

It never came to be. Glantis lifted his dripping body from the waters, cocking his axe back. The axe glowed blue, lighting the entire cave. The warrior threw the axe, letting it fly in a rotating motion from his hand. The magic surrounded the axe as it flew on a direct course toward the serpent. The axe struck the beast's head, causing a brilliant blue flash. The magical power enveloped the creature, burning the very scales of the serpent to ash. The beast thrashed back and forth in agony. Within moments, the serpent's charred flesh and body fell into the water disintegrating, forming a black pool in the center of the lake. Glantis was pale and fell unconscious, face first, into the shallow water.

Surlonthes stumbled to his feet not believing what his eyes had just shown him. He had seen the whole phenomenon and questioned his sanity. Surlonthes sheathed his sword and raced over to the unconscious warrior, pulling him out of the water and propping him against the rocky wall.

Drek walked back into the entrance, steadying himself with the cavern wall, trying to get over to Glantis. The prince cupped his hands and began to splash cold water onto the warrior's face, shaking him by his shoulders. In a few moments, Glantis awoke, mumbling to himself. Surlonthes helped him to stand. Glantis raised himself wearily to his feet and began to search his surroundings.

"Levantia! Parlock!" Glantis yelled.

"Great god!" Surlonthes called out. Like an untamed animal, the prince splashed through the water. He was half running and swimming toward the limp-looking Levantia. Drek followed while Glantis ran over to Parlock.

Surlonthes kneeled near Levantia, holding her tightly and whispering in her ear.

"Where are you wounded?" Drek asked her, seeing the red water flow around her body.

"My leg," she whispered weakly.

Drek knelt, examining her leg. The wound was in her right calf, apparently cut by a jagged rock. It was deep, blood still gushing freely. Drek placed his hands upon her calf. His hands began to glow red and seconds later burst into flames, fusing the wound. Levantia lifted her head screaming. Seconds later, she fell back unconscious into the prince's arms. Drek struggled with himself, wrenching his eyes closed.

"What is it, Drek?" the prince worried. Drek began to blink trying to lubricate his eyes.

"I have used the magic once too often, thus burning my eyes dry in the search for enough power," the mage said shutting his eyes tightly, slowly recovering. "Don't worry about the girl. The pain is too great to withstand," Drek explained in a cold voice. "She will gain full consciousness in an hour or so." Drek pulled some cloth from a secret pocket inside his robe and quickly began to bandage Levantia's calf. Carefully, Drek and Surlonthes lifted her up.

They were surprised to see Glantis standing behind them holding a limp-looking elf in his arms. The bowman's face was drained of life. His once green and silvery complexion was now colorless and pale. Parlock remained unmoving in Glantis' massive arms. From the look on young Trefmore's face, the companions sadly judged the elf dead.

Levantia squinted. Her delicate eyes shut out the brightness of the fire. Slowly, they adjusted to the light and she began to look around. The last thing she remembered was blue sparks of energy surrounding the serpent and the sweet whispering of Prince Surlonthes. She now looked upon the same cavern where they encountered the serpent. She rested at the entrance, huddled in blankets. A small fire burned a few feet in front of her. Levantia saw yet another light on a large rock protruding from the lake. Three figures stood in front of the rock.

"To the elven bowman, Parlock, I ask the gods to take his soul to the final resting place. As the fire grows weak, Parlock grows stronger." Drek spoke these words of wisdom as Parlock's funeral pyre burned. Only when the flames were finally out did Drek cease to speak. All of them had missed the chance of truly knowing the elf. He was silent and always seemed far away. Parlock was true to his lord and risked his life to save his people.

Glantis alone had heard his last words. He stood in silence thinking of what the elf had said in his final moments: "Let my sacrifice be for a reason, Glantis. Use your god-like powers to banish the evil for all the children of Brendonia. And, if you ever need an elf's help, follow the greenest path." With those words and a brief smile, the young elven man passed on.

"Why me?" Glantis asked himself. "I have a power I cannot control, a father and mother I have never known, and a past as unclear as the future."

Glantis flinched as Drek's bony hand fell upon his shoulder. Surlonthes was also surprised by the mage's other hand. Glantis rose to Drek's touch and slowly walked to the entrance. Surlonthes sheathed his sword, standing up to follow Drek. They all sat down at the entrance around the fire. Glantis began to cook some of the food he carried in his sack.

"How much time until Janestin strikes?" Glantis questioned Drek, while preparing the food.

Drek answered in a harsh whisper, "I cannot be sure, though I estimate we have a good six to eight hours until morning."

Levantia strained to sit up. Glantis handed her some food, and she slowly began to eat. He also handed some to Surlonthes. Glantis did not bother to offer any to Drek, knowing he rarely ate.

"I'll take first watch," Surlonthes stated, finishing his food.

"No need," Drek retorted. "I don't require sleep at this time. I will wake you all in four hours to find the druids' dam."

The four of them agreed, and three of them drifted off to sleep while Drek gazed into the vibrant fire, his dark pupils reflecting the flames.

✦ ✦ ✦

Sounds of clashing steel echoed throughout the cavern.

"Glantis, wake up!" Drek yelled, rolling the heavy warrior over on his back.

Glantis woke up and began frantically packing his gear. Drek roused Surlonthes and Levantia. The prince quickly packed and helped Levantia to her feet. They all lit their torches from the dim-burning cooking fire. Afterward, Glantis splashed water on it from the pool. The group then began to follow the sounds of fighting. Drek led them around the lake to another dark tunnel.

"Glantis," Surlonthes gasped, pointing into the lake. Glantis turned around, staring in amazement. A quarter of the way in the pool was an object glowing blue. Glantis slowly waded out into the water. He reached down and grasped the object. He raised his right hand from the water. It was his axe. It was shimmering bright blue as Glantis Trefmore held it. The blue light faded, and only the light of the torches reflected off the silver blade. Glantis was relieved that he had found the axe. He had thought it long gone into the depths of the lake.

The party dismissed the axe and darted through the tunnel toward the battle. They ran through the caverns following both the light and the sounds of battle. The party came upon an incline leading upward into a lighted opening. The group moved up to the opening, coming to a dead stop. They stood on a high ledge. Glantis stared at the giant cavern. Huge holes in the ceiling fully lit the area. The new morning sun cast golden rays of light, causing the rushing water below to sparkle. There was a cool draft blowing in from the cavern's ceiling. Small pieces of straw, among other debris of sticks and rubble, fell from the jagged ceiling, which seemed as if it didn't belong there. Despite the noise of rushing water, the sounds of ringing steel echoed throughout the cavern. Many short figures in brown cloaks ran about. Glantis looked upon the gnarled faces of the druids. He was enraged as he watched two of them cut the throat of an elf with sharp daggers, the sight reminding him of Parlock.

"Those are bardes. They are born into slavery in the druid culture. They are sometimes known as workers," Drek spoke loudly over the battle's noise. "They willingly work to serve their masters of the higher class. They are nothing for us to worry about if confronted with one or two," Drek paused, tightening his flowing black robes. Then, while pointing a bony finger beyond the bardes, he began to speak again. "Look to the left, there, near the exit tunnel. The tallest of that group are the vates, sometimes referred to as prophets or seers, and in druidic language, it means *followers of the dark one*. They can work dangerous magic." Drek stared at the group with a look of warning.

Glantis gasped in horror, seeing Janestin and his men surrounded.

"There they are!" Glantis pointed. "They need our help."

"We'll have to find another way down," Surlonthes answered. Glantis ignored Surlonthes, watching the sheer horror of battle. He had never seen so much death. The bow-strings of the elves sung, striking their targets with pinpoint accuracy, while the Brendonian army hacked down groups of bardes with weary, sword arms.

"There are too many!" Glantis yelled, feeling his blood begin to boil. "Janestin is heavily outnumbered. He cannot retreat because the druids are blocking the exit!"

"This tunnel, here, might lead us down to them," Levantia shouted.

"No time," Glantis answered back. Glantis Trefmore, axe in hand, leaped off the ledge with a battle cry.

"Crazy," Surlonthes scowled in admiration. The last three members looked over the ledge. Glantis plunged into the deep water. As he hit bottom, he felt his powerful leg muscles wrench under the pressure. His thick thighs absorbed the massive shock. Pushing off the bottom, he rocketed to the surface. Surlonthes, Drek, and Levantia stared in amazement as the god-like warrior shattered up through the water's surface.

"To hell with it," Surlonthes said to himself, leaping off the high ledge.

Disgusted, Drek helped Levantia down the other tunnel, taking the sensible route.

Glantis struggled to swim to the river's bank. He caught some rock and pulled himself out. Trefmore's arms bulged as he lifted himself out of the fighting current. Soon, Surlonthes found himself in the same position. Glantis saw him and ran along the riverside to help. He grabbed the prince's hand, pulling him free of the river's hold. Surlonthes breathed heavy. He had jumped into a deeper area and never touched the river's bottom, forcing him to hold his breath longer.

"Are you ready, boy?" Surlonthes said, referring to the battle before them.

Glantis nodded, readying himself for an attack. Seeing the four bardes running his way, Surlonthes unsheathed his broadsword. With one sharp sweep, two bardes fell silent to the prince's blade. Glantis easily terminated the others. The two warriors fought their way toward the Brendonian army. Still unseen, they ducked behind some rocks, waiting for a chance to change the outcome of this battle.

"We've got to make a breach in the druids' men so the army can escape. We need to get reinforcements before there is nothing to reinforce," Glantis panted.

Sudden, loud blasts off to their left distracted the two men. Fire shot from the mage's bony hands, singeing all that stood in the tunnel's doorway. Drek helped Levantia through the tunnel's exit into the open cavern. Again, the weary man had to call upon his powers to fend off small bands of druid workers. To Drek's relief, Glantis and Surlonthes ran to their aid, killing off the almost defenseless bardes. Seeing no hope in unblocking the Jade River, the party moved toward the exit to the forest.

Drek pushed Glantis out of the way. Looking desperate, he tried to call up his deathly flames. To his despair, he was too late. The powerful vate had already raised his hands, magically sending vast amounts of stone and rubble toward them. The deadly rocks inflicted pain on the party, causing the four to fall into the rushing river. The current pulled them through at high speeds. All of them were too weak to escape the river's death grip. Glantis weakly opened his eyes with a half-smile. Janestin and a majority of his men had broken the druids' circle and were retreating into the safety of the forest. Glantis and the others struggled to stay afloat. They all looked upon the river's edge in horrific fright. Before them waited a giant dark pit of swirling water. Without a fight, the forbidding hole swallowed up the small group. They grabbed at whatever they could, whether it was each other or a trusted weapon. The whirlpool dragged them under. After a certain point, they became unaware of the water. All was a white void of nothingness.

CHAPTER 5

A BIG AND LITTLE HELP

A SMALL, SKINNY FIGURE ran through the forest at a frantic pace. His excited, frenetic speed blew his brown robes about, causing the small runner much awkwardness. As he slipped between branches, some caught his robes, causing him to lose balance. Then the trees got the best of him, forcing him to crash to the forest floor. The tiny barde stood up again looking back in fear. No one seemed to be tracking him.

"Ha, I knew it!" he told himself. "Not even an elf could track me. Only a true druid could find his way through the Ancient Woods, especially at night."

The barde slowly gathered his robes around him and began walking north toward his master's keep.

"Those travelers will pay for what they've done!" the angry barde rasped, thrusting his tiny fist up to the night sky. "They'll pay."

Less than an hour later, the haggard-looking barde made his way into the outer edges of a town. Kratz was the twin town of Partha, located on the opposite side of Black Water Lake. Partha and Kratz were ancient towns. Their time of construction dated back to the rise of the first Druid Order.

The exhausted barde weaved between houses and various storage areas. He laughed as he passed the prison cells, spying two dwarves huddled in the corner of the cell. Before he passed, he spit into the cell. "Ingrates, you're lucky we let you live to work for us," the horrible barde spoke with a devious smile.

Two other bardes on guard laughed aloud at their humorous friend. The small druid worker greeted the two guards asking them something. The guards quickly pointed to a dimly lighted house to the right. The barde thanked his friends and walked toward the home. When he came to the door, his black heart began to beat. Before he knocked, the door opened, revealing a man twice his height.

"What is it, worker?" the vate looked down upon him with disrespect. This treatment was normal in the druid culture and accepted by the barde. He had been born into the third class and was unable to comprehend magic.

The vate became impatient, raising his hands as if to strike out with magic.

"Wait! I have news of intruders," the frightened barde blurted out. The vate's expression changed, and he bid the druid worker inside.

The sky was gray due to an overcast of clouds. The Ancient Woods of upper Brendonia were dead silent. Not a single animal stirred throughout the forest. No birds chirped and no bugs buzzed. The only signs of movement were in the cities of Partha and Kratz. While groups of green-robed vates held council, nefarious bardes whipped and ordered the enslaved dwarves to work. Some dwarves served the families of bardes, while others gathered wood from the forest for the whole community. The majority of the dwarves were forced into the remaining Kantar Mountains from the continental divide. There, the dwarves extracted precious metals from dangerous mineshafts and then transported them to the tower of Quin to be melted and molded into swords and supplies. Day after day, the same thing occurred throughout the druid kingdom.

To the east of Quin stood the keep of the druid highmaster. The Ancient Woods surrounded it like a mother cradling her baby. After the highmaster's keep was built, it was said that the trees rooted beneath its walls and secured the keep into the forest floor. Even on the brightest of days, the high-stretching trees encased the keep in an impenetrable darkness. The Druid's Keep was constructed with the heaviest of stones. Not even an ounce of sunlight ever touched its chilling walls. Its color was shadow black. The keep was said to be alive. Legend said a low-toned hum emitted from it. Each sound would penetrate the infinite thickness of the walls. Slowly it would beat, creating an eerie sound. It was a heartbeat. The drumming sound was slow and forbidding. This was the heartbeat of highmaster Bernac himself.

Many legends told that Bernac was abandoned as a child. Some said that he was born of two vates, a forbidden consummation due to the dangers of mixing two magical half-bloods to create a full-blooded druid. This was forbidden under druidic law in order to avoid the chance of one druid being more powerful than that of the other druids. Although the reasons for his birth were unclear, the one fact remaining was that one of the most powerful vates in the druid culture raised Bernac. Hate and resentment filled Bernac. He eventually learned his caretaker's magical arts and murdered the very vate that raised him out of love. Many believed that Bernac was evil from the beginning of his birth. Others speculated that his anger toward the very parents that abandoned him made him bubble with hate. This inward struggle was so powerful that it eventually lashed out onto anyone that crossed his path. His power was so strong that he was able to gain control over all the druids. Even the vates together feared his wrath.

Bernac sat upon his cold throne, meditating to the sound of his black heart. The highmaster was wrapped in the blackest of robes, his eyes unmoving and dark. He was deep in meditation. Hatred filled his druid body.

The throne room had a gray color about it. No light was in this room. Not a single torch hung on the wall. If any other than a druid would enter the castle, he would see nothing but utter blackness. Despite the darkness, the druids could easily see. This room, like most other rooms in the keep, had no decorations or lighting. The walls were made of gray stone, turned black from existing in the darkness for many years. The keep's solemn purpose was to shade the highmaster himself from the harmful sunlight. The more Bernac was exposed to the sun's rays the more his lifespan decreased. He was the last of his kind, the last true druid living. Although the vates were strong with magic, nothing compared to that of the highmaster. As for the bardes, they were almost human, except that their night vision had twice the clarity.

The upper floors of the keep were different. Some areas had window-like openings to let in the sunlight. These were the druid prisons. The highmaster often locked bardes up in these rooms for making mistakes. The sunlight would torture the bardes. It was not really that the sun's rays were harmful to the bardes, but more like a mental torment because of their love for darkness and preference to be out of the sun's rays.

A barde entered the throne room.

"Highmaster Bernac," the barde addressed and bowed. "There is a vate from Kratz here. He claims he has news of intruders."

Bernac's dark face hardened with anger. "Bring him in, now!" the impatient druid commanded.

Briskly, the green-robed vate walked into the room. He immediately bowed to his master.

"Master," he rasped, "forgive me for my tiredness, for I left Kratz last night and was forced to travel the last few miles in the light.

"What of the intruders?" Bernac hissed.

The vate caught his breath and then spoke. "Last night a barde from the tower of Esu traveled to Kratz and spoke with me. It seems four human intruders fell into our magical hole in lower Brendonia and somehow survived the trip to Esu. The intruders apparently killed several bardes and are currently traveling toward the dwarven city of Lore."

"Do they have any help from the dwarves?" Bernac questioned.

"No, Master, but the bardes did not follow them into the dwarven territories."

"What!" Bernac rasped standing to his feet.

"Master, I assure you, they are not a threat," the vate stuttered.

"I will be the judge of that, vate," Bernac scowled. "They must not be allowed to leave upper Brendonia. Block off all ports, and set up lookouts everywhere."

"Should we intrude on dwarven grounds, Master?" the vate asked.

"No, it is not likely they will leave at once. The fools will likely try to discover our plans. If they are humans, like you say, they will most definitely try to help the dwarves," Bernac said with a crooked smile. "They must have been part of the force that attacked our stronghold in the Kantar Mountains in lower Brendonia. That fool Hestin is falling for it. Vate! Double the speed of the shipments and supplies to the tower of Quin. Ship more troops to Fos. Tell the other vates that as soon as the majority of the king's army leaves, attack Castle Brendonia at once."

"Yes, Master," the vate bowed leaving, "I will not fail you."

"You had best not, for I will be watching through your eyes," Bernac threatened. "Halt!" Bernac hissed. "I will return you to Kratz."

Bernac walked in front of the vate. The master druid raised his hands. He began to make signs and murmur magical words. The vate's body transformed into a blackish gas and dispersed into the air.

Water poured from the magical hole encased in the stone ceiling. The hole was bright white, but its light began to flicker. The white light flickered from a bright to a dim radiance. Next, the water ceased to pour from the breach in the ceiling. Seconds later, a heavy object blasted out of the hole.

Glantis Trefmore instantly regained consciousness as he fell toward the ground. With a heavy thump, he landed onto a wooden gutter. Glantis grasped the edge of the gutter, restraining himself from sliding down the steep-angled shaft. Looking up at the hole, Glantis let out a sigh of relief. This feeling turned to anxiety as he recognized the broad body of Surlonthes falling straight toward him. With a sharp heave, Glantis jumped off the side of the gutter, landing feet first on the ground below. The constructed gully was not very high, only about as high as his chest. Surlonthes landed hard, the wooden supports shaking beneath his body weight. Glantis grasped the prince's cloak both catching and pulling him off the gutter. Before they could speak, the two warriors witnessed Levantia and Drek falling from the hole. The mage screeched painfully as he hit the slippery shaft. Levantia's body came out next, crashing down on Drek. Glantis and Surlonthes pulled them easily over the side and brought them safely to the floor.

The four looked up in wonder at the bright hole and the mysterious contraption in front of them. A partial answer came as they watched massive quantities of water blast out from the once dry hole.

"This wooden gutter must channel the water somewhere," Drek deduced. Before the group could internalize Drek's words, a door off to the left burst open.

"Intruders!" a brown-robed figure screeched from the doorway.

The party unsheathed its weapons. Glantis swore in disgust. He must have dropped his weapon while falling. Then, as if the magical hole inscribed in the stone ceiling was the answer to all their problems, his silver, shimmering axe fell from the hole, sticking into the wooden gutter. With the grin of battle on his face, Glantis grabbed the axe by the handle, tearing it free from the wood.

Druid bardes spurted through the doorway in many groups of two or three. Glantis pushed Drek aside, seeing he was still weak from the previous fight in the caves. Drek did not seem to care, for he turned to Levantia and helped her back to a safe position.

Surlonthes was already near the door slashing the hordes of cloaked figures from side to side with his heavy broadsword. His sword was unforgiving in its bold attacks, cutting down the helpless-looking figures. Glantis, too, was fighting off the bardes, both chopping and kicking them down. Only one barde remained at the door. Surlonthes raised his sword and swung it down; however, the frightened barde jumped out of the way. The barde ran away from the tower down into the Ancient Woods. Surlonthes raised his sword yelling and mocking the defeated druid.

Surlonthes jumped back from the door, and his yelling ceased. "I don't think I should've done that."

Bardes began to swarm the tower, having heard the unfamiliar voice yelling. The companions soon found themselves overwhelmed. The room rained metal blades. With great repetition, the bardes threw varieties of small knives and daggers at them.

"Fall back!" Glantis yelled to Surlonthes. The prince quickly backed up to where Levantia and Drek stood, sheltered under the gutter structure.

"Get into the gutter. It's the only way out!" Glantis directed, holding the druids off until the last member of the party was in the gutter. When he saw his friends slide down the channel, he dove upward into the wooden gutter, its destination unknown. Just as Glantis jumped, one of the barde's daggers pierced into his left arm, but then fell out. Thwarted, the bardes exited out the door from which they had entered.

The watery path was fast and direct. They slid on and on, carried by the swift-flowing water out of the building. They all began to tense up, seeing the end of the gutter. It was too late. It was impossible to stop. Glantis watched his friends go speeding over the edge. As a last resort, Glantis swung his axe into the gutter bottom. No luck, the axe's blade would not bite into the wood enough to hold him. Glantis soon flipped over the edge along with the water. He fell fifteen feet until he splashed into the water head first. When he resurfaced, he dizzily looked around for his waterlogged friends. They all swam to the shoreline, removing their heavy packs from their backs. Then they all looked up and studied the gutter channel.

"Look," Levantia said pointing to the top of the gutter, while leaning on Surlonthes for balance. They all followed the wooden structure above them. It stretched from the shoreline up a steep hill to a giant stone tower.

"Esu, the druid tower," Drek answered all their thoughts. "This wooden gutter carries our drinking water to this cove, King's Cove to be exact. The druids are pouring our precious freshwater into this saltwater cove," Drek finished.

The group barely caught their breath as bardes scrambled to the hilltop. Having easily identified the intruders, the druids began to work their way down the hill.

Glantis shouted, "We must swim across!"

With regret, they all reentered the water, dragging their packs with them. "Drop the packs. Carry only your weapons," Glantis gurgled, his bag's extra weight submerging his mouth beneath the water's surface. They all obeyed, yet their weapons still weighed them down. Surlonthes helped Levantia swim, her leg still causing her considerable pain. Glantis, however, was in the worst shape of all. His swimming slowed. His axe was the heaviest of all their weapons. Great pain burned in his left arm as saltwater washed into the open wound caused by the dagger. The warrior's other hand held Drek afloat, who was exhausted. Glantis wondered what it was that drained the mage.

The companions forced themselves to swim the width of King's Cove. Their only focus was on the approaching shoreline. Luckily, by the time the bardes reached the bottom of the hill, they were out of range. The bardes were running around the cove's shoreline. The companions reached the shoreline none too soon. Any longer of a swim and they all would have drowned. The party sprawled upon the muddy beach sands.

"Follow me!" a strange voice said from the forest. "The bardes are running around the cove. They are almost on top of us."

Suddenly, Drek rose, his robes now permeated with water. Exhausted from his overuse of power in the Kantar Mountains, Drek's face expressed utter hatred. The mage raised his bony hands, this time forcing the power to flow through his fingers. "You shall pay for this!" Drek aimed his hands at the hundreds of bardes running toward them. After swimming the lake, the mage's mood had turned stale.

"No!" Glantis leaped to stop Drek, pulling his hands back over his head. "You will kill yourself. You're too weak." Glantis helped Drek into the forest. The party ran at a slow pace; the great weight of fatigue was relentless. The dizziness began to flow into their heads while their hearts beat to the cadence of galloping horses. Glantis' eyes began to blur as he smashed through thick brush, clearing the way for the others. He could only see that the person he followed was very short, stocky, and carried a weapon almost as big as his body. His quick pace was killing them.

The stranger slowed to a walk. "I think we've lost the weasels, no thanks to all your pokiness," he squawked.

Glantis opened his mouth in protest, but the small man cut him off.

"Silence, ya big fool, or they'll find us."

Glantis lowered his head in silence. "What is it that causes me to obey this stranger?" Glantis pondered.

Surlonthes smirked, seeing the annoyed expression on Glantis' face. They followed the small man through the quiet forest. The sun was down, and it became impossible to see. Yet the stranger led them on, unaffected by the low light. They walked a little under an hour. The companions seemed to drag their bodies along. Then, out of nowhere, the little man led them into a clearing. It was a quiet town with only a few homes lit by candles. A few small fires blazed in the center of the town. Groups of small men gathered around the fires.

"Welcome to the dwarven town of Lore," their guide spoke up. "I am Grey Thornstar, the last descendant of my royal family. I'm like a king among my people."

"Thornstar, are you talking to the trees again? You crazy old dwarf," another dwarf yelled, overhearing from a short distance away.

Grey disregarded the comment and continued. "I am sure you have heard of me. I am a great hero known among all the dwarven people." The dwarf babbled on and on about adventures and his great courage. Too tired to listen, the companions just followed without protest. The promise of rest was all that kept them moving. The dwarf snuck them unseen into his home. The house was barely taller than Glantis. The doorway was less than five feet high. Both Drek and Levantia followed with not much trouble while Surlonthes and Glantis had to squeeze their way through the dinky doorway.

Grey seated himself in his beloved rocking chair. He rocked, stroking his sheep-white beard. From what Glantis had observed so far, most of the dwarves looked the same. Each had a dark beard matched with black eyes. Grey was different only in that his beard was white.

"I am an old warrior, probably the eldest in this town, what's left of it." Dismissing his thoughts, the dwarf turned his head and looked over the group. "What are your names? How did you get yourselves in that tower without being seen? What do you know?"

Drek, reviving, explained the whole situation to Grey. This was no risk considering that before the continent's partial division the dwarves were strong allies against the druids. Drek explained their plight, careful to leave out certain things concerning Glantis. Surlonthes looked at Levantia's leg wound, and Glantis rubbed his left bicep looking for his wound. To his amazement, not even a trace of scar tissue remained. Drek finished the tale and in no time, they all fell asleep, Grey having been already asleep. Drek, however, rubbed his eyes, still stinging from his overuse of magic. With a bony hand, he reached beneath his robes, pulling up a talisman from his neck. It was a gold chain wrapped several times around Drek's neck. It had a ruby center. A dragon's claw grasped the stone with its golden talons. The ruby flickered strangely with a dim light. Drek's eyes squinted in surprise. He did not recall the talisman ever glittering with light. As the light faded, Drek realized the talisman must have been what he'd felt earlier burning his chest. He remembered a distinct heat in his breast when he was near the river blockage in lower Brendonia. Drek wondered what the glowing could mean. The mage dismissed the idea, closing his eyes to regain his strength in meditation.

"Wake up!" Grey pounded his mace upon his home's oak floor. "In my youth, I slept five hours on average and woke up before dawn."

All but Drek, who was already up, awoke groggy. Glantis could feel his muscles tighten and spasm as he moved. Forgetting the low ceiling, Glantis stood up.

"Ouch!" he groaned as he rapped his skull against the ceiling's rafters, mumbling something about little dwarven homes. Glantis and the others grabbed their weapons and exited the claustrophobic home. The morning's fresh air revived their spirits. Drek and Grey stood waiting outside, watching the dirty companions seep out of the doorway.

"Come, we must hurry before my village awakes. There is no time to explain to my people about your quest. We must leave unseen, or we will face too many questions. Besides, the dwarves here are just a bunch of goons anyway. I promise clothes and plenty more food when we reach Dry Rock." Grey passed out small containers of water and small helpings of meat. The companions, except Drek, all gulped down the food in appreciation. It had been a little less than a day since they had food or water. One thing entered all their minds: they owed many thanks to the dwarf who had both saved and sheltered them.

The five of them walked south out of the village. Grey had told them of a secret place called Dry Rock, where the dwarven resistance gathered their army. "Just south lies the canyon. It is there that we'll find Dry Rock. We should arrive well before nightfall," Grey explained.

"What is happening on this hellbound continent?" Surlonthes demanded of the dwarf.

"I shall tell all. When I speak, keep your disrespectful, ox-tongued mouth closed," Grey said with great authority, raising his heavy green mace.

Surlonthes drew his sword. "We shall see who will have a tongue!"

"Prince, sheath your weapon! Our war is not with the dwarves," Levantia spoke from behind, still walking with a limp. Surlonthes obeyed, dismissing the dwarf from his thoughts, stepping back to help Levantia. They were all a little on edge from the stressful journey.

"The lady speaks with intelligence, for she knows a great dwarven warrior like me has defeated knights twice your size and courage," Grey said, lowering his mace.

"Why you old dwarven fool, you couldn't cut your way out of a fishing net," Surlonthes reprimanded.

"Enough!" Drek rasped. "Tell us of the druids."

"As I was saying, before I was interrupted," Grey glanced at Surlonthes, determined to have the last word. "There are, as you probably have seen in the Kantar Mountains, many druids. They are mostly bardes, I would guess, from the descriptions you've given me. The bardes are slaves of the vates and the druid highmaster. They accept it honorably, and fortunately, for us, they make up the vast majority of the druid population. The bardes are very weak fighters but can be very damaging in large numbers." Grey glanced at Surlonthes when he said the word "weak." The prince did not notice. He was helping Levantia along since her leg was still in the healing process.

"Anyway, the vates are the worry. As you have all seen, they can use magic strong enough to wound or kill. We will need to be cautious when dealing with them. The druid highmaster we cannot fight alone. His magic is of an incomprehensible power. It will take a strong force to get close to him. We have found one weakness. It's nothing much, I tell you. It's simply the sunlight. Only the six vates who exist and the highmaster himself are affected by the light. If exposed for long periods, they begin to age fast. The bardes appear unaffected by this. They are not magic users of any sort. They are more human in nature, bred small by their master."

Grey began to speed up the pace. They quickly came to a wall of brush. Grey pushed through it. He then sat on the ground and slid down out of view. The others followed. Behind the bushes was a steep incline where a slippery trench wore into the hillside. When everyone reached the base, Grey stopped a moment. "This just helps conceal the direct route to Dry Rock. If this path is not taken, one would have to take a longer route around all this brush and these brambles, risking capture."

They all started southwest again. Grey soon continued. "Remember this. At night is when the vates and sometimes even the master druid himself stalk the lands around us."

"Who is this master you speak of?" Glantis questioned with interest, wondering if the dwarf knew anything of Bernac.

"The highmaster, my friend, is just as his title suggests. He reigns and rules the Druid Order. Unlike all other druids, whose identities are considered insignificant, the highmaster has a name. He is called Bernac. My people suspect him of the continent's division. Bernac and his six vates call themselves the Council of Sinx. They wish to rule all the land in the north and south.

"How did you come upon this information?" Surlonthes asked, still somewhat annoyed and suspicious of the dwarf.

"Many of my people, as you know, have been enslaved. Over the years, we have helped some escape. Several had been in contact with Bernac himself. A small number have even seen him. They have captured and killed thousands of dwarves, many of my own bloodline." Grey fell silent putting his mind on the trail.

The group saddened, looking at each other. The companions were surprised to see Surlonthes' eyes moisten.

After a long moment of silence, Grey spoke again. "If you look far to the east, you will see a pass lodged between the mountains. This, my people call the Darkpath. It is the only way into the Ancient Woods from this side of upper Brendonia."

"Why is it called the Darkpath?" Levantia said, struggling along the trail.

"It's only a few miles to Dry Rock. I will have my friends look at that leg wound of yours," Grey said, noticing her limp. The old dwarf then began to answer her question. "We call it the Darkpath because of what's on the other side. Druids, day-in and day-out, keep a never-ending watch for dwarves. The Lord Bernac has issued us a warning never to enter the Ancient Woods for any reason. If caught, we face a lifetime of enslavement."

"Then why cross in the first place?" Levantia questioned.

"Precious metals and food are scarce in these parts. At one time, my people had many mines in the Kantar Mountains. At one time, we would gladly trade precious metals for food with the bardes beyond the Darkpath. Now their ways have changed under the new ruler. Bernac and his vates are controlling them all. Bernac has poisoned their minds through glorious tales of one day ruling all of Brendonia. He tells them that they will spread their population across the continents and become the strongest race ever known.

"What are the druids doing with your people?" Glantis came up alongside the quick-paced dwarf.

"That's easy, lad. They're working them ragged in the mines. I've watched with my own eyes. They extract ore in massive amounts for the metal."

"Where do they take it, Grey?" Glantis persisted.

"It is taken to the tower of Quin, about twenty miles southeast of here, just beyond the Darkpath."

"There's another tower?" Drek showed a sudden interest.

"Yes, a newly built one like that of the Druid's Keep," Grey answered.

"Keep? The druids have built a castle?" Drek's voice was louder than any time the companions had ever heard.

"Nothing to wrinkle your robes over, mage. Quin's construction began after the division of the continent. The elders know more than I of the fortress."

Changing the subject, Glantis asked, "What do they do when the ore is taken to Quin?"

"Ah, now that is worth talking about, warrior. This is a mystery to the elder dwarves of Dry Rock. The druids ship all their metal out to sea. The strangest part is that they head toward lower Brendonia, but as you said, there are no signs of ships sailing toward the south. Some of our best mapmakers have charted their course. It makes no sense. The boats seem to be heading nowhere, yet somewhere, for each ship follows the exact course," Grey reached up scratching his head. All became silent. The companions walked, all wondering about the druids' behavior. The day began to darken as the old dwarf led them on. The more Grey said, the darker it became.

An hour before sunset, the weary travelers carried their tired bodies down the last slope. From what Grey was telling them, Dry Rock's entrance was somewhere at the base of this gorge. The terrain was much drier in this area. Animals became scarcer here. No matter what time of day, it always remained very hot in the canyon.

Glantis had taken notice of all the landscapes on this journey. He was aware that the forest was very dry, similar to the forests of lower Brendonia. "Does it rain much here, Thornstar?"

"Rarely, my boy. I can tell you that it rains like clockwork just beyond the mountains. Whenever the Ancient Woods become dry, it rains." Grey stopped, looking all along the gorge's high ledges, now above them. "This way, my friends." Grey led them to a wall of steep rock. In front was a clump of bushes. Grey, stepping up to the shrubs, pushed them aside, to reveal a black opening. "Go, quickly, and don't worry, the tunnel will get larger," the old dwarf laughed a bit.

Drek entered first, and then Glantis squeezed his way through. Next, Surlonthes helped Levantia in, following behind her. Grey backed into the tunnel watching the gorge's ledges for spies. Seeing nothing, he quickly let the brush retract over the hole's entrance.

CHAPTER 6
THE DARKPATH

"WELCOME, THORNSTAR, what news do you bring?" an extremely old dwarf called out in a cheerful voice. The dwarf's hair was completely white with a matching beard that extended all the way to his waist. He stared at the companions with dark eyes. On both sides of him stood much younger dwarves. Each had jet-black hair and looked very fit.

"I have brought people from lower Brendonia. They are from King Hestin's army. I found them running from 100 or more bardes up near King's Cove," Grey answered, motioning the companions forward. Glantis and the others bowed. They all stood in a dome-like structure. Three levels of ledges wrapped around the dome walls in a full circle. Every level contained many doors either closed or open in which one or two dwarves were either entering or exiting. The brilliantly crafted dome looked like a complex beehive. The pounding of iron echoed throughout the dome. Everywhere dwarves worked constructing everything from beam supports to swords and shields. The dwarves were no small people except in size. They excelled in the areas of ingenuity and artisanship. There was no question whether a dwarf could work or not. It was commonly known that a dwarf, male or female, matched the stamina of two humans.

"Let us get away from this noise," the old dwarf stated. They all followed him through another tunnel into a quiet room. The leading dwarf told his guards to wait outside while closing a cloth curtain behind them. The room appeared empty of life. Then a dwarf stepped out of a shadow along the back wall.

"I, friends, am Gullon, war leader of this hidden city. Who have you brought here, Grey?" Gullon asked. "Are these truly friends of King Hestin?"

"The boyish-looking warrior is Glantis. In the black robes is his caretaker, Drek. The woman Levantia is held by King Hestin's daught...son, the Prince of Brendonia, Surlonthes." Grey looked innocently at the prince. Surlonthes sneered at the old dwarf. He then looked to Gullon and nodded.

"Praise the gods!" Gullon yelled out unexpectedly. "Help has finally arrived. I take it the king received one of the letters?

I welcome you. Sorry there is nothing for you to rest upon," Gullon said, looking at the weary travelers. He then pushed the curtain aside motioning for someone. Two dwarves peeked around the curtain. "Bring each of these men temporary clothing and food. Take the woman to see what the medicine man can do for her leg." The two dwarves scurried in and took Levantia out of the room. "It was rude of me to ignore your tiredness. I apologize. My mind is elsewhere, but I'm afraid time is something we don't have. Now, tell me all you know," Gullon asked with a welcoming smile.

The conference ran well into the night. In those hours, the warriors ate and changed into long cloaks. The companions were all very tired but were thankful toward Grey. The old dwarf did most of the explaining by retelling the stories he had heard from Drek in his home in Lore.

Gullon explained that to launch a proper offensive he would need more dwarves. Gullon's plan was to secretly go into the druid cities and break out all the imprisoned dwarves. If it were at all possible to get more men, they would have to try to get them. Gullon presumed the best way to help the dwarves escape successfully was to have them flee to King's Cove and swim across it. This idea he got from the companions. Gullon thought once they got across, the group of soldiers posted at Lore could help fend off an attack. Finally, both armies from Lore and Dry Rock could form a strong offensive at the Darkpath.

It sounded entirely all too easy to Glantis and the others.

"Too unpredictable," Glantis thought to himself. "The chances of success are almost zero." Many thoughts ran through the warrior's head. He concluded, however, that this is what he had strived for when he joined the Brendonian Legion. He remembered what Golis had said in the valley about learning to use his powers. The power had surged through him more than once, and if anyone was capable of this task, it was he.

"Come in," Glantis groaned at the noise of the loud rapping on the door. Startled, he opened his eyes, awaking with strength.

"Get up. It's almost midday. If we are to be ready for our journey, we need to be preparing now," Grey spoke in a loud voice.

Glantis jumped out of the bed still wearing the cumbersome robes. "Good morning, Grey," the warrior said smiling. "I feel great now that I've had a full night's rest."

"Here are your clothes. They've been sewn and cleaned anew." Grey smiled, his old face wrinkling. The old dwarf held a pile of clothes, stacked up just under his big nose. Glantis began to laugh at the sight of him. Grey soon followed, laughing with his strange cackle saying, "Hurry and take your clothes from the top before I fall over."

Glantis took his clothes. Grey left the room to deliver the others to his friends.

The companions all met each other in the soldiers' eating hall. Chattering dwarves filled the room. All of the companions had overslept but were now bright-eyed and ready for travel. There was a special table for them set up by the soldiers. Grey told them this was their way of showing appreciation. Glantis and his friends smiled, thanking all the dwarves they passed on the way to the table. The companions all sat down, surprised at the comfort of the hard, wooden seats.

"Midday break!" Gullon shouted over the noise, walking up to sit down in the remaining chair. The companions all turned, surprised at his sudden appearance. For an old dwarf, the eldest in the population, Gullon surely did not show it. Before anyone could speak, friendly dwarven folk brought great amounts of food and drink to the table. They all ate heartily, filling their empty stomachs. Drek, of course, had nothing. Knowing Drek was some sort of a mage, Gullon thought it best to accept his eating habits.

As the majority of them finished their meals, the low humming of the break bell sounded. Amazingly, the dwarves quickly finished and scurried back to their workstations. Only Gullon and the group remained in the eating hall.

Gullon snapped his fingers, summoning a dwarf carrying a rolled parchment. Gullon took it from the dwarf and sent him off. Gullon unraveled the paper with his thick, gnarled fingers. He revealed a map of upper and lower Brendonia, clearly showing the division.

"So, as you say, there's a magical passage from the lower Kantar Mountains to our upper Kantar." Gullon ran his fingers from one area to the next. He looked over the map not expecting an answer to the statement.

"From what I saw at Esu," Drek broke the silence, folding his robes, "the magic was a reflection of light used as a means of teleportation."

Gullon put his hand upon his rounded chin, pondering the idea. Accepting it, he looked up. "We all know the plan from last night's conference. If any of you wish to back out say so now. You won't be looked down upon for your decision. I can send some of my best dwarven soldiers. We can replace some of you if we must. It will be understood." Gullon looked directly at each one in the party.

Levantia cleared her throat and spoke her feelings for the group. "We went to the Kantar Mountains to unblock the Jade River and destroy the druids. Even if strange workings of magic brought us here, it doesn't change our situation. We came here as a team, all with the intentions of helping. Be assured that none of us will back down," Levantia told Gullon.

"Very well, you are all brave warriors, but remember your main purpose is to free my people. This must be clear. I'm sure we can regroup and perform a proper attack on these death-faced druids." Gullon quickly rolled up the map, putting it into his pocket. "Follow me. I want all of you to see our progress."

They all followed Gullon from the eating hall.

Drek looked with surprise at Levantia. "You're not limping, how?" The mage stared at the healed wound, immediately thinking of Glantis' healing abilities.

"Our medicine man knows a bit about 'magic' himself, mage," Gullon smiled.

Drek remembered Levantia leaving with the two dwarves. The mage was relieved to discard the idea of her having the healing powers of Glantis. "A ridiculous thought," Drek told himself. As for the medicine man's 'magic,' he probably used some sort of healing root from the Ancient Woods.

"Be sure to thank him for us all," Surlonthes pressed.

They quickly walked on and closed the matter. Soon ringing sounds from the dome reached their ears. In moments, they walked into the giant room. Dwarves ignored their presence, busy working to make their deadline. Gullon led them to giant tables, showing them the huge quantities of weapons and supplies.

"If the dwarves you free make it to Lore, they will have enough weapons. That, I'm personally making sure of," Gullon said as he waved his hand over a table filled with weapons. Gullon grabbed one of the hammers and began to bang it against the table.

"Attention!" Gullon bellowed.

His strong tone of voice surprised Glantis. Grey had told him that the elder was close to 150 years old.

His voice was strange. It echoed throughout the dome. "I'm sure the rumors have already reached your ears, but let me make it clearer. These five brave souls, including one of our own kind, Grey…" Gullon blushed, looking toward Grey for help.

"Thornstar," the old dwarf grumbled.

"Yes, yes, Grey Thornstar." At this, Grey raised his heavy mace into the air, stunning the dwarves into a mixture of confused murmurs and mild cheers. Grey lowered his mace, emotionless.

"I thought everyone loved and respected you, Grey," Surlonthes jested. Grey ignored the prince and pretended to be interested in Gullon's speech. Seeing the little dwarf's reaction, Surlonthes placed a supportive hand upon Grey's shoulder.

"They will travel through the Darkpath to the cities of Partha and Kratz. Sometime in the next few days, they will attempt to free our people so that we may regroup and crush the druid forces." At Gullon's end, the dwarves yelled, holding up their tools in a battle cry. The dome echoed shouts and hollers. Gullon waved stepping down from the table.

The dwarven leader proceeded to lead the warriors into smaller tunnels away from the main dome. "We have prepared several years for this attack. I don't have to tell you dwarves are impatient. Hatred for the druids runs deep in their blood.

The druids have almost destroyed our way of life. Only the thoughts of revenge keep my people from giving up."

"Where are you taking us?" Glantis asked.

"To the outer east wall where you can leave unseen," Gullon explained leading on.

The tunnel they traveled down had torches on every wall along the way. After they reached a certain point, Gullon pulled five torches from the wall, handing one to each. On the way, Gullon explained the need for them to find a hiding place during the day in order to see the druids' encampments.

When they finally reached the end of the tunnel, Gullon handed them a sack he was carrying. "Inside this is four day's food. That should be enough to travel to the cities of Partha and Kratz." Gullon gave them each a strong hug wishing them a safe journey.

Gullon grabbed Grey whispering with purpose, "You will be well commended for this, my brother."

Grey seemed to brighten up after this comment, standing up, perhaps, a little straighter.

Gullon beckoned Glantis to his side and motioned for help pushing the wall at the end of the tunnel. Glantis walked forward laying his hands upon the wall, pushing. The wall began to creak and screech. Slowly, light began to fill the tunnel, causing them to squint. A cold wind blew through the tunnel. The companions marveled at the construction of the large door. It had been practically invisible.

Saying farewell for the last time, the travelers wrapped their cloaks tightly about them and stepped outside. They found themselves behind a group of thick bushes again. While the others pushed through the shrubs, Glantis helped seal the door. Before it finally closed, he heard the muffled voice of Gullon, "Good luck, brave warriors."

The night came quick. The companions were huddled behind a small ledge just behind a large hill. Just below the hill extended the Darkpath. Drek watched the pass for hours, not a single druid appeared.

Now the five of them sat eating around a warm fire.

"You best put out the fire, Glantis," Drek told him. "Even behind this hill the glow might be seen."

Glantis filled his hands with dirt from the ground. He doused the fire with sand, quickly extinguishing it. The group began gathering their supplies. Since no horses were available, they tossed away anything not vital. This made the packs more bearable to carry. The party climbed up over the ledge gathering at the top of the hill. It was now pitch black out and it was impossible to see. Visibility extended no more than ten to twenty feet in all directions. They all looked at each other. All of them decided that since Grey knew the way, he should lead.

"Ready?" Grey looked upon Glantis and the others. They answered by unsheathing their weapons. Levantia, hungry for revenge, pulled out her short sword. Surlonthes, at her side, revealed his broadsword. Glantis held up his axe as he followed Grey, who still carried his cumbersome mace. Drek looked about them, and then slowly followed from behind. All were silent as Grey led them down the steep hill. The entrance to the Darkpath stretched before them.

Grey led them sure-footedly down the hillside. The warriors followed behind, covering their bodies from sight behind thick tree trunks. The group infiltrated the Darkpath. Tree by tree, they slipped deeper into its domain.

Minutes later, the group heard movement other than its own. Glantis caught his breath as the others did. Strange as it was, Glantis felt his heart beat faster the deeper they descended. Glantis and the others hid behind five trees, not more than three feet away from each other. A mere twenty feet in front of them stood a small group of bardes. A strange thing happened at this moment. Something Glantis would never forget. As the five warriors hid behind some tree trunks in the midst of darkness, the four of them turned to Glantis. The young warrior was astonished seeing his companions looking to him for direction. Glantis took a deep breath. With a serious look and a hand motion, he led the attack. The companions one by one moved from their positions. Glantis went first, while the others followed in amazement.

Glantis sprinted toward the bardes, faster than any man in Brendonia yet quieter than a light breeze.

"In the name of...," Grey spoke to himself, "he cannot be human."

Stomping his thoughts flat, Grey went second. Surlonthes, Levantia, and Drek scattered out, attempting to surround the unsuspecting bardes.

The bardes looked up at the sight of Grey charging toward them. Before they even drew weapons, Glantis swung his axe from behind. The killing stroke of Trefmore's axe literally ripped through three bardes, causing fatal wounds. In moments, Grey's mace hit another in the face, sending the druid lifelessly to the ground. Next, Surlonthes hacked the remaining barde with a swift stroke of his broadsword. In a matter of seconds, the five bardes were slaughtered. Levantia and Drek had not even the chance to fight. At this moment, Glantis did not see the eyes upon him. He felt them. He knew he was different. He knew what he had done. The skill seemed to appear out of thin air. Only this time it manifested itself at his will. For not a human alive could swing any weapon with enough force to penetrate three men. Glantis ignored the stares and walked on. The companions snuck through the Darkpath. An eerie silence spread across the Ancient Woods.

"Usually the bardes crowd this area," Grey whispered. The others agreed. Something was wrong. They all decided to stray from the path's opening back into the forest. In moments, the companions ran back onto the path.

"Bardes!" Glantis warned as he led the group back onto the path.

Hundreds of bardes now jumped out from both sides of the path. The only way was forward. Knowing it was a trap, the companions ran hard hoping to outrun the bardes. Their worst fears surfaced when bardes appeared in front of them blocking the path.

"Keep running!" Drek yelled in a piercing tone. With a raise of the mage's bony hands, flames burst into the night air. The bardes in front of them lit up like fireflies. One by one they fell. While running hard, Glantis looked over at his foster father. Seeing him slow, Glantis scooped him up off the ground, carrying Drek's fragile body forward. Everything was a blurry sight as bardes screamed from behind, while others burned ahead. The enemies were getting so close that Levantia and Surlonthes were constantly facing bardes.

Then, as if a thick, black smoke from a fire had descended upon them, everything turned dark. All movement stopped. In what seemed to be moments later, they found themselves surrounded by angry looking bardes. The five of them stood motionless in a circle, their weapons cast down in front of them. The companions' hearts beat as they found they could only move their eyes. The strange part was that they were completely conscious. They stood motionless for minutes at a time, straining to look at each other, but their sights directed forward as a cloud of smoke gathered. A forbidding black gas emerged before them and evolved into the shape of a man. Glantis squinted, trying to judge who or what it was. Finally, the man took full shape. At that same moment, they were free to move.

"Bernac," Grey said in awe.

"Very good, dwarven scum. I thought your kind was not able to distinguish gender, let alone faces," the strange man spoke with a forbidding smile. The group stood in wonder, now able to move, yet not wanting to.

Bernac, the druid lord, stood before them.

"I must confess. This group is quite surprising. You've succeeded in escaping my bardes once. Feel free to thank them. Because of their mistake at Esu, I now stand before you." Bernac ground his teeth together looking at his bardes with a sarcastic smile.

"Restore the continent, druid!" Glantis spoke boldly, ignoring Drek's warnings.

Bernac's attention immediately turned to Glantis. With an extremely pleased smile upon his face, the druid stepped closer. "You wish to speak, fool?"

"Yes, Bernac, I command you to release the dwarves in Partha and Kratz. I command you by the authority of King Hestin to remove your clan from the Kantar Mountains," Glantis finished, his voice unwavering in speech. Once again, he was feeling the energy flowing within him. He was no longer afraid of the druid that stood directly in front of him.

Bernac, feeling quite disturbed by these comments, stared into Glantis' eyes. "What is your name?" he requested.

"Glantis Trefmore," Bernac's voice hissed aloud, reading his thoughts before Glantis could reply, "You're a fool who laughs at death."

The druid lord backhanded Glantis. The warrior collapsed heavily to the ground. The others dared not move, knowing it would be useless. Glantis shook his head, slowly regaining sight and consciousness. A sudden chill overtook him. He was scared because the power he had possessed earlier was gone. Bernac stepped closer to him, and to the others' surprise, Glantis scurried back like a frightened field mouse.

"I'm afraid I cannot grant your request, warrior." Bernac knelt closer to Glantis and displayed a sarcastic, saddened face. He then raised his body up and laughed. Glantis, still on the ground, covered his ears. The laughter seemed to tear into his soul.

The druid spoke, "Know my power, Glantis, and do not forget it." Bernac turned away. Then he spun around to say something more. "Oh, and I will grant you something." There was a slight pause. "You and your friends shall watch each other's flesh rot off under my lock and key!" With that, Bernac walked off, turned toward the group, and raised his hands as if casting a spell. The bardes watched as the bodies of the one called Glantis and his friends dispersed into a dark smoke.

King Hestin stood upon one of the castle's towers, gazing up at the night stars. Hestin pulled his thick cloak about him, warding off the chilling night air. "Five nights since they left, where are they?" Hestin questioned himself. The king looked out onto the dark grasslands. He searched for a sign of his friends. Hestin longed for his son's return. Like any father, he would not rest until Surlonthes came home. The king slowly strode over to the tower's opposite wall. He now watched over the New Sea. The crescent moon glowed, casting a dim light upon the water.

"My Liege, I have news from both Janestin and Vincent." A tall, skinny man walked onto the tower.

As Hestin turned to greet the messenger, a sparkle of light glittered from the New Sea. He jerked his head back searching the sea's horizon.

"See something, Sire?" the messenger questioned.

The king turned back saying, "What news do you bring me?"

"Yes, Sire," the man jumbled through his pockets until finally revealing two letters. He quickly unraveled one of the parchments rereading it. He then looked up to the king to summarize.

"Janestin explains that the first attack into the Kantar Mountains was an utter failure. The druids dug in more than imagined. They need troops desperately in order to launch a counterattack."

"Read the other," Hestin stated.

The messenger obeyed, opening the second letter and reading it verbatim:

"My Lord Hestin, the gnomes aren't cooperating. They refuse to support the kingdom with their water source. Gnome troops are stationed from Kylar all the way to the southern side of the Moonpool. The gnomes are surrounding the last of Brendonia's freshwater. As you know, the gnomes are a primitive and stubborn race.

I'm in need of a few hundred troops. I'm sure my men can break their defensive and take temporary control of the Moonpool."

Commander Vincent

"Take note of this," the king said. Hestin pulled his heavy cloak around him once more. He trusted Vincent, knowing that in these last few days the commander tried his best to persuade the gnomes to help. He agreed. A temporary control of the water was necessary. As for Clifford Janestin, there was no doubt upon his word. Janestin was not one to waste the lives of others before his own.

The messenger rolled up his parchments, fumbling to place them back into his pocket. He pulled a piece of blank parchment from his tunic. The messenger rummaged through his pockets once more, looking for a quill.

The king looked at him with irritation. "On your hat."

The messenger turned bright red, slowly reaching up taking the quill from his hat. The king masked a smile and then began.

"Janestin, I shall indeed send you the troops, but I can spare only a small amount. I must take precaution for an attack on the castle. When this letter is in your hands, the troops will arrive one day later. Send word immediately if anything occurs."

The messenger quickly jotted down the king's last words onto the parchment. The king waited for him to finish and then gave out his orders. "Send another 500 men to the elven city of Torka. Send the same to Commander Vincent at the gnome city of Kylar."

The messenger quickly rushed down the stairwell to deliver the orders.

Old King Hestin walked the tower once more looking in all directions. To his surprise, he thought he saw another white twinkle upon the sea. Attributing the idea to his imagination, he left the tower.

CHAPTER 7
THE DRUID'S KEEP

"LOOK WHAT YOU'VE gotten us into," Grey's voice echoed in the midst of darkness. "If I was leading back there, none of this would have happened. If I had my weapon back there, I would have struck down Bernac myself."

The companions sat on a cold, stone floor confused. They seemed to be ignoring the old, fitful dwarf. Their eyes were finally beginning to adjust to the darkness. They were locked in a cramped, cold, and damp room. A draft blew into the room from under the doorjamb. Slowly, the warriors moved together in a small circle, hoping to create warmth. Tiny holes lined the west wall, allowing a little light to seep into the room.

Glantis felt a pain inside him, remembering the deathlike touch of Bernac. Despite having no scars upon his face, somehow a scar remained. The infliction, however, was not visible. It dwelled in his soul. Glantis had never felt anything of this nature. Until now, nothing had really damaged him for long periods. As a child, he remembered his injuries always healing quickly. The injury inflicted by the barde's dagger in the tower of Esu had also healed quickly, too quickly. An injury that otherwise would take months from which to recover, took mere hours to heal. Yet, something was different about Bernac's cold touch. It made Glantis feel mortal. His strength and energy felt almost completely drained. Although the event took place hours ago, somehow the warrior could not break free of its cold grasp.

The others worried about him, seeing his leadership and motivation diminish. The companions had seen many things from the warrior that were not within the capabilities of a human. They had seen powers unknown to them. Even though they could not understand it, when Glantis used his powers they felt a sense of goodness pass through their inner being.

Silence monopolized the room until an aggravated Grey burst out, "Let's break out of here. Obviously, the druids are not going to feed us. We have been left here to perish in the darkness. Place your ear against the door. Nothing, you will hear nothing!" Grey said hysterically.

"What do you suggest we do, dwarf?" Surlonthes raised his voice in anger.

"Break down the door is what we'll do!" Grey retorted.

"What do you mean *we*, Grey?" Surlonthes questioned, hiding his smile.

"Surely you don't think I can do it alone, being of old age," Grey said with utter sincerity.

Glantis stood up. "What do we have to lose?"

Surlonthes saw the look of seriousness on Glantis' face and shrugged his shoulders. Ignoring Grey, the two heavy warriors readied themselves, as the others moved to the outer walls. With a husky order from Grey, Glantis and the prince rushed the door. The two forces connected with the wooden door with a large thump. The only other sound was the roar of the two men. Both Glantis and Surlonthes rested, propped against the door, unmoving.

"Have another go at it. I'm sure I heard the locks creak," Grey explained.

The two men backed up rushing the door again. Once more, the door gave out a loud, yet solid, thumping sound.

"Again!" Grey commanded. "Why, in my prime I could have easily torn that door from its very hinges, single-handedly."

"You couldn't—," Surlonthes began, but stopped seeing Glantis readying for another run. At last hope, they rushed into the door at full strength. Defeated by the iron bindings and the hard oak, the warriors backed away from the solid door. Surlonthes sat down next to Levantia clutching his sore shoulder while Grey slid his back against the wall until he sat on the chamber's stone floor. The dwarf wore a look of hopelessness.

Drek motioned and spoke to Glantis with a gasp that seemed filled with pain. Glantis kneeled down next to his foster father. Drek clutched his black robe tightly about his thin frame. Ever since his arrival into upper Brendonia, Drek's physical appearance showed signs of deterioration. In the past, whenever the mage exhausted himself, due to an overuse of magic, he had always quickly recovered. After the fight in the Darkpath, Drek became extremely weak. Worse yet, when they were teleported to the Druid's Keep, Drek seemed to be suffering from some sort of massive energy drain, while the others were virtually unaffected. The only real difference was that he was not recovering.

"How do you feel?" Glantis asked in a worried tone.

The mage then murmured in an undertone, which only Glantis could hear, "As you can see, I am in no condition to use my powers. Even if I could, Bernac cast a spell upon the door that will absorb my magical flames as harmlessly as water," Drek ended his sentence in a painful gasp.

"How do you know a spell was cast upon this door?" Glantis questioned.

"Before you and Surlonthes rushed the door, I attempted to burn it, but the door absorbed my magic."

Glantis gave him a look of disapproval. "You shouldn't have exerted yourself. We can always find another way out," the warrior paused, his face becoming flush with anger. "Did the druid place a spell on you as well?"

"No, my energy loss is caused by something else," Drek whispered.

"What is it?" Glantis persisted, staring directly in Drek's eyes.

Seeing the look of worry in Glantis' eyes, Drek quickly responded. "Worry not, Glantis, I will survive if we can manage to escape and get as far as possible from this place," Drek barely finished being so short of breath. He rested a bit and then spoke again, his voice hardly audible. "Many times, my son, have I seen your god-like powers. Do not let the druid take away your faith in yourself. Seize your fears. Control your thoughts, and you shall prevail. Only your beliefs have limits, not your strength."

Glantis clenched his fists, gritting his teeth behind his lips. The great warrior closed his eyes, searching for the inner-strength he possessed. Something barred his way from calling upon the power. The coldness he felt would not permit the power to flow. Just when it seemed the magic would appear, his thoughts would deviate to the horrors Bernac had placed in his mind. The druid had drained all his confidence. Somehow, his mind's balance tilted. Glantis lowered his hands to his sides, unclenching his fists. It was useless. It was now beyond even his power to open the door.

A distant voice entered the warrior's mind: *"Are you done? Do you give up? Perhaps I've made a mistake."*

Glantis looked up, scanning his friends' faces for affirmation that they also had heard the voice. To his disappointment, none showed any sign of hearing anything.

Who had shown disappointment in him? He was sure the voice had neither come from any of his companions nor was it Golis', the forest master from the Valley of Soul. Perhaps it was Pantos. No, that was impossible. He wanted to impress the voice that had spoken. Despite not knowing the speaker, he somehow felt an obligation to the unknown person.

Glantis lowered his head concentrating deeply within his thoughts. A bit of magic began to flow within him, and instantly the power overtook him. He had done it. He had broken through the barrier. The coldness no longer threatened his inner being. Bernac's hold on him was broken.

The others looked up, watching in amazement. Glantis was now glowing. A dim blue light bubbled around him, forming around every curvature of his body. The same glow that surrounded his axe in the caverns, returned. With an amazing charge, Glantis plowed his right shoulder into the impenetrable door. The door broke loose, amid the sounds of creaking hinges and bolted locks ripping out of the stone walls. The door smashed to the ground, vibrating the stone floor.

Grey, being the quickest on his feet, ran out the doorway to help Glantis up from the debris. Glantis stood up, blinking in amazement at what he had done. He had totally freed the iron locks and hinges from the wall. Some of the hinges had several pounds of stone still clinging to them. Glantis succeeded in breaking two oak boards that ran across the door frame.

The others came out. Levantia and Surlonthes were helping Drek, the mage, still exhausted for reasons unknown to the companions. The others did not notice, but Drek had a sly smile upon his face when he saw Glantis' great feat of destruction. At the same time, the mage noticed that part of his talisman was visible. The large, red ruby, surrounded by a golden dragon claw, began glowing bright. Drek grasped at it in disgust, placing it deep beneath his dark robes. It was glowing brighter now. "Perhaps it glows because I have never used my power to such extremes before?" Drek wondered to himself.

As Glantis reflected upon what he had done, his self-esteem was elevated. The cold depression he had felt diminished. Even now, his hands glowed with a blue aura.

They now stood in a dark hallway that seemed to open up to the left and right. What waited beyond, however, was unknown. A mist of darkness obstructed any further sight in both directions.

"We need light if we're going to escape the Druid's Keep alive," Surlonthes warned his companions.

Grey searched the floor until he found what he was looking for.

"What are you doing, Grey?" the prince grumbled.

Grey began to pull some bandages out of his pockets. The dwarf was wrapping them around something. Next, small sparks of light flashed as Grey struggled to light his improvised torch.

"Stand away. I will light it," Drek announced in a wavering voice.

"No need for magic, mage. I have it under control," Grey told Drek.

They all waited several minutes as the dwarf sparked his flint, the torch not yet igniting. Then the torch caught flame. "You see? No need for magic, just a little patience."

The rest of them began to pick up pieces of wood from the shattered door. Grey passed out more bandages, and soon they had three torches, each giving off a sufficient amount of light.

"You see, just patience, mage, that's all," Grey pressed.

The five of them ran down the hall. It was strange that they did not see any guards.

"They must have suspected the room to be impossible to escape from," Glantis said, giving voice to their common thought.

Abruptly, a sharp humming buzzed in the warrior's ear.

"What is it, Glantis?" Levantia asked, seeing the glazed look across his face.

Glantis did not respond. The troubled warrior turned his head trying to locate the source of the noise. He walked further down the hall. As he peeked around the corner, seeing it to be clear, he waved the others to follow.

"Where are you taking us?" Surlonthes questioned, walking up next to him.

"I don't know," Glantis answered, paying minimal attention to Surlonthes. Before the prince could react, Glantis took off again. Surlonthes motioned the others to follow. Surlonthes struggled to half carry, half drag the drained mage as Glantis led them down many empty hallways and corridors.

It seemed the lord druid Bernac had underestimated them and now considered them as good as dead. Strange enough, the place was deserted. There was no sound or activity, and yet Glantis seemed to be following something.

After a few minutes of searching, they stopped. The warrior stood trance-like in front of an ordinary wooden door.

"What the—" Grey started to complain before he was cut off.

"—Do you hear it?" Glantis asked expecting agreement. The humming was so loud in his own ears it was difficult to believe only he could hear it. Glantis reached out and pushed the door open. The room was not a room. It was a small storage area. Glantis lifted his torch above his head, lighting the closet. The companions all gasped as Glantis removed his shimmering axe from the room. In the warrior's giant hands, the axe glowed in the low light. Glantis stared in awe as he watched the blue glow slowly diminish. Then, as if waking from a daydream, with swift hands Glantis began handing back the confiscated weapons. Surlonthes grasped his broadsword, placing it in his empty sheath. Levantia took comfort in the return of her trusty short-sword, swinging it through the air twice before nimbly sheathing it. The last weapon Glantis pulled from the small room was a heavy, battered, green mace.

Grey grabbed his mace in astonishment. "How did you know our weapons were here?"

Glantis reached up and scratched his head. "I don't know really. I just followed the humming of the axe. Once I grasped it, the noise stopped, as if it were calling me."

The companions all looked at each other in bewilderment.

The silence broke with the sound of footfalls coming toward them.

"Let's move," Glantis said as he closed the storage door. The footsteps were becoming louder. Glantis and the companions ran down the hall. Seeing his foster father having problems, Glantis supported him. The two ran together down the cold hallways. More often now, their roles were changing. He was now giving support to Drek.

Levantia and Surlonthes ran alongside the old, gray-haired dwarf. The two watched Grey, speculating about the little man's past. On this strange journey, Grey was an utter nuisance, yet a vital helper. He was now part of the illustrious group.

The honorable companions came to a corridor. Their choice was either right or left. Glantis turned to the group, and again he found it strange that they all looked to him for a decision.

"I have failed them once already," Glantis thought, watching their trusting eyes. With a broad smile of love, Glantis chose left, and as the companions strode left, several bardes jumped out of the right passageway, an obvious ambush. The quick-footed bardes were catching up, and the companions were forced to turn and fight. Grey threw his torch at the advancing bardes.

The druid creatures did not slow, easily dodging the torch. The bardes had their swords out and were ready for combat.

Levantia, being in the rear, found herself engaged in battle first. Surlonthes drew his broadsword as Levantia stabbed the leading attacker.

Four bardes remained, each attacking at once like a pack of hungry wolves. Forced to stand in the rear, Glantis saw a haze of brown robes rushing in toward them. The prince easily took down two of them and Levantia another. One remained, who was swinging at Levantia without warning.

Grey Thornstar's mace came out of nowhere blocking the barde's downstroke, allowing Levantia to stab the last druid. The crazy dwarf was kneeling upon the floor between the prince and the woman warrior.

Laughing, Surlonthes pulled Grey up by his collar using only his left hand. Grey reacted by placing the end of his mace to the ground and resting both hands on the handle, smiling as if it were nothing.

"It was the only way I could get between you two from back here." This time the whole group laughed. Even Drek showed signs of laughter. They were laughing in a time of utter seriousness as a way to dispel the tension of the moment.

"Come on, we're not out yet," Glantis reminded them. Again, all followed the giant warrior into an open room at the end of the hall. Unlike the other areas, a window-like opening let in light at the far end of the wall. The dim outer light showered in, lighting a spiral staircase leading down. Glantis led them down the staircase. They guessed this to be a tower, judging by the rounded walls. To their dismay, this was no exit from the castle, just an open doorway leading into yet another castle room.

Glantis looked frustrated. "Wait here," he told his friends, "and stand away from this wall." The confused companions stood away from the solid stone, cylindrically shaped wall. Glantis quickly took the stairs, taking three at a time. Soon, he was out of sight. The companions sat at the bottom of the stairs, commenting on his strange behavior.

Glantis reached the top of the stairs, and standing before the open window he looked down at a 100-foot drop to the ground. Glantis looked in front of him. A large tree branched out more than forty feet in front of the window. Glantis strapped his axe to his back, then bravely perched himself on the ledge of the window. He slowed his breathing and his heart. He looked up into the dismal skies, high above the trees of the Ancient Woods.

"I am not of this world. I know I do not belong here," he thought. "I, alone, have been placed upon this world to face the evil that threatens it. What happens if I resolve this struggle? Do I die? Will I be able to live normally?" Glantis stood hunched in the window, now staring at the distance between him and the far tree branch. He then spoke aloud.

"I ask the god. I ask my real and true father to help me control this power. Of what use is it if I cannot help my friends? Do not fail me, father." It was with those last words that Glantis leapt. As the great Trefmore hurled himself forward, his body and soul glowed blue like the sea on a sunny day. Through the air the weightless warrior flew. As if time were pausing, Glantis approached the tree. It was within his reach. With an inhuman grip, Glantis grasped the rough tree branch. The old tree bent low, his heavy body posing a threat to the survival of the aging branch. The great force caused his body to move like a pendulum. The warrior gained his balance and control. Then, like an animal of the forest, Glantis jumped and swung from branch to branch. Perfect accuracy brought him rapidly down the towering tree. As Glantis came to a controlled stop on the tree's lowest bough, he dropped thirty feet to the forest floor. He touched the ground feet first, feeling on impact the weight of his axe pressing upon his broad back. He let out a painful growl as his legs resisted collapsing from under him, but it was not surprising that the inhuman muscles once again held up against the awesome force. Regaining his balance, Glantis ran toward the tower wall where his friends waited within.

Bardes swarmed the staircase, and still no sign of Glantis. Levantia was holding them off at the entrance. Every time the warriors killed one, five more appeared.

"Use your magic, Drek!" Grey screamed at the mage.

"No need for magic, dwarf, I'm sure you'll think of something. God knows you've the *patience*," Drek hissed at the dwarf's command.

Grey was suddenly sorry for what he had said to the mage earlier about patience.

The black-robed mage shot extremely wide streaks of orange-red fire killing many bardes. After a few weak shots, Drek collapsed from exhaustion, falling to the hard floor. Grey and Surlonthes held the staircase. One after another, bardes fell, bloodstained bodies sprawled over each other.

"How many are there?" Surlonthes remarked, not expecting an answer.

The fighting stopped as an alien noise penetrated the air.

Glantis Trefmore swung his blue shimmering axe at the tower's outside wall. The powerful blue glow had spread from his hands to his axe. Glantis transformed energy into physical strength with his mind. With each second that passed, the magical strength increased. Again, the sound was heard as the silver axe penetrated the wall creating a hole large enough for the dwarf to fit through. Again, Glantis struck the cold stone of the Druid's Keep. This time the whole tower began to tremble. The companions helped to enlarge the hole from the inside. When it was large enough, they scurried through the hole. The first thing they saw was the god-like Glantis towering above them. The warrior stood with his blue eyes focused on all of them. They watched his axe and body shimmer bright blue in the evening light. As the magical aura diminished, it enabled Glantis to assume his normal composure.

Bardes began to appear from the crumbling tower by way of the hole Glantis had made.

"This way." Grey motioned, running clear of the tower. The bardes were now approaching them, their numbers ever increasing. The companions looked behind them. The tower shook and rumbled. Then all at once the castle's left tower fell in a great crash. Heavy rock from the falling tower showered the bardes less than ten feet away. The hardened stone smashed many of the bardes, killing them. In a matter of seconds, the entire left tower covered the forest floor in small and large piles of stone.

The companions were now almost 100 yards from the Druid's Keep. As they looked behind them, they saw many bardes attempting to follow, but soon aborted the action, acknowledging defeat. Too many of their brethren were dead and buried under the keep's stone.

The little company raised their hands yelling in victory back at the bardes. "We sure left them a mess to clean up," Grey remarked, turning back to look. "I thought those stone blocks looked a bit brittle," Grey continued, always having an explanation for anything he did not understand.

All their thoughts veered toward Bernac. Would he try to find them again after learning of their escape? Soon, hard running ruled out any conversation. The priority now was to conserve energy. They ran following Grey deep into the forest. The old dwarf had traveled these parts many times and knew the route. The victorious companions were now running toward the druid city of Partha.

The sun had long since dropped behind the horizon; however, the full moon provided some light for them. The companions now traveled along Pauper's Road, once well used by the king for transportation of supplies throughout Brendonia, now an all but obliterated trail, overgrown and rugged.

"How soon until we reach Partha?" Glantis asked the exhausted-looking dwarf.

"Not soon enough, I'm afraid, at least not in time to free my people tonight." They all remained silent, walking steadily along the trail. The night's breeze was nonexistent. Seldom would the travelers enjoy its comfort. Since night had come, the sounds of the forest ceased. It seemed as though nothing wished to reveal its position. Grey led the group slower now, his exhaustion becoming more apparent. All of them were a little edgy, looking back at imaginary sounds and jumping at druids that turned out to be mere shadows.

"Let's rest here," Glantis called out to Grey. The tired dwarf turned around and saw an expression of worry on the boy's face. The little man then glimpsed Glantis motioning to Drek with surreptitious eyes. The mage, who was usually so strong, now walked with a clumsy step, but still wore a stoic look upon his face. It was odd seeing Drek so exhausted. Ever since they reached upper Brendonia, he seemed different. The mage overused his powers before, but always overcame it with a few hours rest. Grey, unaware of this, took Glantis' expression seriously and stopped.

"We'll never make it to Partha at this pace," the dwarf grumbled under his breath.

Surlonthes and Levantia, on the other hand, were silent since Glantis destroyed the tower. The two seemed to be growing fond of each other, whispering and smiling. Perhaps they needed something to get their minds off the journey. The two fighters kept falling behind the rest of the group. Even Bernac's evil powers couldn't stop two people from caring for each other.

Once under the opaque cover of the towering oaks, the moon's silver light faded. They huddled closer together for warmth, not daring to light a fire. They all had lost their packs, probably given to the bardes by Bernac. Seeing everyone's face with the look of hunger upon it, Glantis began to go through his pockets. His giant hand revealed a bulky leather case. He unfolded the leather and produced several large pieces of dried meat. His hungry friends voiced their surprise.

"Where did you get the food?" the little dwarf asked, speaking for the rest of them.

Glantis looked at his friends. "I always like to keep a snack handy when I travel," the warrior said.

His friends burst into laughter admiring his appetite. Glantis began to laugh, too. "I wanted to save it until everyone began to really weaken. Only problem was, I got hungry first," he smiled. Again his friends laughed, only this time with food in their mouths. They finished the last of the food and all tried to get a few hours sleep.

Glantis opened his eyes to an annoying, squeaking sound. He reached to his right, grasping his axe. He stood up, his eyes searching the old Pauper's Road. A fast-moving cart rumbled down the trail. Two horses pulled it. From what Glantis could see, only a single, small man drove it. The cart came fast and would soon pass them by. It was traveling toward the Druid's Keep. The cart was full of supplies, probably from the twin cities of Partha and Kratz. Glantis strapped his axe to his back and ran toward the trail while the others remained asleep. The warrior ran with great speed and stamina. He wanted to intercept the cart before it passed. If he missed the cart, he would never catch it.

The cart's wheels raced along with the gait of the horses. Glantis' powerful legs strode across the forest floor, his muscles flaring out from the shock. The cart was inching by him. There was no chance to intercept at his present pace. The struggling warrior pushed himself hard, knowing if he obtained this cart, they could save the dwarves this very night. To Glantis, this meant maybe saving one more life or preventing one more dwarf from punishment. All these thoughts and more passed through his mind. With this, the mysterious, god-like strength returned. The giant warrior began to glow blue. At first, it was dim, and then it intensified. Glantis concentrated on reaching the cart. Faster and faster he ran, a blue streak of light shooting out from the forest onto the trail. The warrior leapt and landed squarely on the cart with his axe raised high, shimmering blue in the night's sky.

As the screeching noise increased, the others began to wake. Not seeing Glantis, they gathered their weapons and ran to the trail.

To their surprise, they saw a man struggling to turn a horse-driven cart on the narrow trail.

"That's Glantis!" Levantia raised her voice above the noise. The companions ran toward the cart.

"Run! Hurry," the familiar voice of Glantis bellowed. The companions learned of the danger. A whole horde of bardes was converging on the cart while Glantis struggled with the cart. He was able to turn it and command the horses forward. The bardes were right behind him. Some that Glantis had not seen when he jumped on were hanging onto the back of the cart. In moments, the bardes began to succeed in slowing the horses because of the resistance they were causing with their feet.

Grey Thornstar ran fast, even with his heavy mace and his short legs. The old dwarf was leading his friends. Levantia, running right behind him, screamed out trying to draw the bardes' attention to them. Surlonthes lagged back, helping the struggling Drek.

There was no way his friends could catch up to the cart. Glantis pulled on the reins, commanding the two horses to turn off the trail. As the horses responded, the cart jerked and jolted on the rocky terrain. He knew the cart might collapse, yet this was his only choice. It might just shake the bardes off the rear and maybe his friends could get on.

The strong-souled group reached the side of the cart. Thanks to Glantis, all four of them jumped in, causing the horses to whinny at the increased weight. Levantia and Grey, both breathing heavily, brought their weapons down upon the few bardes still clinging to the cart. With no swords to defend themselves, the druids fell from the cart like drops of water. They all watched as the small company of bardes was outdistanced while Glantis worked the cart back onto the trail.

Drek was motionless in the cart. The wheels hit rocks along the road, agitating Drek's body from side to side. The mage rested in disillusionment, bewildered by the reasons for his weakness. Still feeling this discomfort, Drek loosened his robes. To his surprise, a light shimmered from under his shirt. The black-robed mage fumbled under his shirt, pulling out his talisman. Its golden chain wrapped several times around his neck. The talisman glowed bright. The ruby was a deep, forbidding red that hurt one's eyes if looked upon too long.

"No, it cannot be," Drek whispered to himself, realizing for the first time what the talisman's glowing ruby truly meant. This time there was no mistake.

CHAPTER 8

BLACKWATER

G LANTIS AND THE OTHERS caught sight of the dark town of Partha. Only three hours of night remained. They would have to move fast in order to free the dwarves. Slowly, and as quietly as possible, Glantis steered the cart over to the side of Pauper's Road. The cart's wheels rumbled and squeaked over the rough terrain until coming to a stop. The horses were still panting from the grueling chase by the bardes.

Surlonthes, already out of the cart, stood up near the horses. Unhooking them from the heavy cart, he let them free. The horses whinnied in appreciation as the front of the wooden cart smashed to the ground releasing the great weight from their backs. Grey jolted awake as the cart connected with the hard ground. Everyone was already out of the cart except the dwarf. As Grey crawled out of the cart, he made sure everyone was aware of his disappointment in the cruel joke. The group laughed at the crabby dwarf. As the rugged dwarf stood up, he tried to hide his smile while glaring at all his friends.

The companions were becoming hungry again. It was less than luck that Grey's nose had sniffed out some bread and meat buried in some of the cart's cargo boxes. Inside one of the crates, Grey dug out some backpacks. Having lost their other packs to the bardes, the group sorely needed these new ones.

The companions ate some of the food and loaded the rest into their packs. They gathered their weapons and set out toward Partha.

"How does everyone feel?" Glantis asked looking back at his friends. No one answered. Everyone, even Drek, was walking without any noticeable trouble.

Grey increased his pace to catch up with Glantis. "What does it feel like?" the dwarf asked.

"I thought you believed it to be coincidence," Glantis answered, keeping his eyes on the trail.

The rest of the group crept up around Glantis.

"I don't remember much while it's happening," the warrior spoke in a serious manner. Not looking at his friends, he stared ahead. "But I can now call it at my own will. It seems to increase my strength. It's an aura of power. Only it's good, not evil. Calling upon the power is becoming easier, but controlling it is another matter altogether."

"How does it travel into your axe?" Grey questioned.

"That I am unsure of. I still sometimes wonder how the axe calls me."

"What do you mean it calls you?" Grey persisted.

"Both under the Kantar Mountains and in the Druid's Keep, the axe called to me somehow. First, it summoned me by light and second by sound as if the axe would be somehow important."

The companions peeked at the axe strapped to Glantis' back.

"Another thing I have not told the rest of you is that when I met the forest master, Golis..."

Drek pushed between the others and grabbed his shoulder. Feeling the cold touch of Drek, Glantis fell silent.

Glantis began to think. Maybe it was not right for him to speak about what Golis had told him. Yet why must he keep these things to himself? Brushing these thoughts to the back of his mind, Glantis noticed that everyone was silent. As the big man looked at his friends, they seemed preoccupied. The sound of bardes from the town of Partha broke everyone's thoughts.

By Glantis' lead, the companions ducked into the forest. Again, the warrior found his friends depending on him. "Why me?" Glantis thought. "Last time they followed me, I led them into a trap. I almost got everyone killed in the Druid's Keep."

They traveled as quietly as possible through the forest, the trees black and mystifying in the odd fog that hovered above the forest floor. The companions worked their way from side to side, dodging the thick brush and tall trees. Only an hour or so remained until dawn. They managed to work their way around the town from the outer edges of the forest without being detected.

Glantis stopped. He threw his arms out to stop his friends from moving forward. The warrior wiped his brow of sweat as he looked at the steep incline leading down into a huge lake. "If we'd have fallen in there, the bardes would've surely heard us," Glantis whispered.

"Blackwater," Grey gasped with frightened eyes.

Glantis and the others faced Grey. Surlonthes put his hand on the little man's shoulder asking, "Have you seen this place before, Grey?"

"Only once," the dwarf answered, "when I was here trying to help some dwarves escape."

"Did you break them out?" Surlonthes persisted.

"Oh, I broke them out all right. During the escape, I chose to cross this horrid lake by boat thinking it would be quieter, not knowing what was in its depths." Grey stared into the lake of Blackwater. The lake's water was murky. A blackish mist hung over the lake's placid surface.

"What happened here?" Glantis asked.

Grey's speech slowed and his throat constricted. "I don't know. Something in that lake grabs hold of its victims and pulls them down to their death."

"A forst," Drek's voice hissed from behind them. "A deadly creature. How did you manage to escape it?"

"The vines began to shake the boat when finally the forst, as you call it, capsized the boat. There were four of us. When we fell into the water, I heard muffled screams of a woman and two children as the vines pulled them under." Tears came to the dwarf's eyes as he recalled the horrible night. "I tried to save them!" he cried out. "I did," Grey explained, thinking he had to convince the others. "It was hopeless. Sometimes I wish I'd have died with them. I lost my family that day," he said softly, lowering his head.

The rest of the companions crowded around the dwarf with wet eyes. All of them patted him on the shoulder trying to express their sorrow. At the same time, they admired his courage for joining the journey. Grey had been fully aware of the requirement to return to this horrid place of ill memories.

Glantis grabbed the little dwarf's hands and stared into his eyes. The giant warrior said nothing, yet somehow Grey felt his strength and courage returning. Glantis, however, was angered. Bernac had senselessly cost all the races of Brendonia many lives.

"There's not much time," Surlonthes said, shaking Glantis. The warrior awoke from his trance and looked into the sky. It was still very dark, yet sunrise was less than an hour away.

"Does everybody know the plan? We'll break out all the dwarves and then supply them with weapons, if possible. Next, we'll send them toward Lore by first leading them to Kratz, the twin town of Partha just beyond Blackwater." Glantis bit his tongue for mentioning the lake.

"It's over now, Glantis. It was a long time ago," Grey said.

Glantis spoke, never moving his sight from the dwarf's eyes. "Let's do it, then. For we must not, and we will not, fail. *That*, I know, my friends." Glantis looked upon all of them with an unwavering confidence.

Glantis led them around the steep ridges of Blackwater. Soon they approached the town of Partha. A small number of the houses were lit up, and only small bands of guards walked the dark streets.

"Be cautious in your moves," Glantis whispered, "for they see much better than us at night." The others nodded and began to follow him. The party advanced down the street alongside a string of dark houses.

Glantis and the others ducked between two houses when they saw some bardes headed toward them. They placed their backs to the wall and slowed their breathing. The bardes passed them, engaged in their own conversation. While Glantis and his friends waited for them to get out of sight, he spotted a group of cages. The small prisons were crowded together and located in the inner city. As soon as the way cleared, Glantis led his friends deeper into the town. When they reached the cages, the prisoners shied away.

Glantis grinned wide. "We are friends. We have come from lower Brendonia to free you." This was all he had to say, and the dwarves were up to the bars. Soon the other cages began to shake.

All the dwarves saw Grey and began asking his name. Grey told them a few times. "Grey Thornstar's the name, Grey Thornstar," he finished swinging his mace in a triumphant way.

Glantis gave him a quieting look. The companions began pulling on the cages. The barred doors would not budge. Glantis told them to cease.

"Where are the other cages?" Glantis asked one of the dwarves.

A young, haggard boy came to the bars. He looked over-worked and undernourished. "The rest of the prisons are in the rear of the city," the young dwarf answered.

"Where are the weapons kept?" Glantis questioned.

"The weapons are also in the rear of the town in a separate cage. Oh, and," the young dwarf paused, "if it is possible, my father is being kept in the torture hole. He is very old, and he collapsed two days ago. Since he was unable to work, the bardes put him in the hole. It will take more than ten of us to lift the huge stone cover. I'm afraid for him."

A smaller dwarf appeared from behind his brother. He wore a look of exhaustion with a face covered in dirt. The small child tugged on his brother's ragged clothes asking in a high, squeaky voice, "Is he going to save papa?"

Glantis went into an internal rage when he both saw and heard of these abominable acts. The bardes had placed children no older than six years into senseless slavery. "We came here to break out *everyone*. I will save your father. Do not worry." Glantis stepped away from the bars clenching his hands. He took a quick look around for guards. "The others are being held in the rear of the town," Glantis pointed. "We will have to break these locks with our weapons and guide these dwarves to the rear of the town. This boy tells me their weapons are in a separate cage on the other side of town. As soon as we break these locks, the bardes will hear us. We'll have to run fast to obtain those weapons, or we'll not stand a chance of escaping," Glantis whispered staring all around for bardes. The five companions drew their weapons each standing in front of a cage. Glantis waited as each of his friends told the dwarves of the plan. "Strike hard," Glantis said, giving the signal to hit the locks.

The sound of metal hitting iron clanged into the night. More than once the warriors brought their heavy weapons down upon the locks. One after the other did the iron bindings break loose. Joyous dwarves poured out of the cages in a frenzy of freedom after the warriors broke open the prisons.

Glantis ran to the two remaining cages. Drek quickly stepped next to him. "I can do this. Maintain order in the crowd."

Glantis gathered the dwarves together and led them to the other cages on the other side of town. Meanwhile, Drek turned his attention to the locks. The black-robed mage stretched both hands out holding a lock in each. Drek's eyes flared red as did the iron locks. Within seconds, the locks reached extreme temperatures. At that moment, Drek shook the molten iron to the ground as if it were water. Drek opened the two cage doors and led the astonished dwarves across town toward Glantis.

The whole bunch of them was running to the rear of the town. Soon, the bardes were upon their heels. At first, not too many followed, but then the numbers increased. The escape had shaken the town up a bit. This was to the rescue party's advantage because the bardes were slow to react. The druid henchmen were a few streets behind.

"This way," Glantis said as he recognized the hoard of cages at the end of the street. With great luck, the warrior discovered the separate cage holding the weapons. Glantis sprinted ahead of the group, his powerful leg muscles surpassing the group with ease as if they were standing still. In moments, Glantis closed in on the cage. Before coming to a complete stop, he was already swinging his axe down upon the lock. As the great strength and momentum of Glantis' axe connected with the iron, the lock shattered apart and fell to the ground. Glantis jerked the door open and began throwing the weapons out of the cell. War-hungry dwarves, thirsting for revenge, picked up and handed out swords, daggers, pikes, and shields.

By the time Glantis reappeared out of the jail, the dwarves and bardes were in full combat. Glantis found the little boy and his eldest brother behind him. They were staring at him in silence, waiting for the stranger to fulfill his promise.

"Where is he?" Glantis asked in excitement. The young dwarf pointed to a stone platform covered with iron rings. The two brothers watched the amazing human run off to the site.

Glantis came to the stone cover. The children were right. There were several iron rings spread out on the stone designed for many wooden poles used to facilitate carrying by ten or more bardes.

The two brothers watched as the huge warrior spread his muscular arms diagonally across the length of the long stone cover. Glantis grasped the two outermost rings. He stood hunched there for a few seconds.

"He's not going to try to lift that himself, is he?" the dwarf's little brother asked. The eldest one could not find the words to answer. All he could do was point. The brothers both watched in utter amazement. The huge warrior was glowing bright blue. The light spread to the stone cover. With a sudden jerk, he pulled the heavy stone slab loose and lifted it above his head. It was an awesome sight as Glantis Trefmore threw the giant stone cover.

An old, weak man looked up in astonishment. "Who... who are you?" the old dwarf asked. The two brothers immediately appeared behind Glantis.

"Father!" the little one cried out.

Glantis grabbed the old dwarf. As he helped the man out of the hole, a strange blue glow shot through the dwarf's body.

"Glantis Trefmore is my name. Follow me. I am here to help." Glantis did not notice, but the old dwarven father had been extremely ill and was dying.

The two brothers hugged their father. Before following Glantis, their father paused saying, "He has the power of healing."

"Is he a god, father?" his little one asked.

The only answer the curious dwarf got was, "We will follow him anywhere."

When Glantis returned to the battle scene, the dwarves were losing by a small margin. Drek was tiring again. The mage was overusing his powers fending off barde attacks. His friends were also tiring. Surlonthes and Grey were leading an attack on a new group of bardes that had appeared from between two houses. There seemed to be too many, causing the prince and dwarf to retreat.

Levantia also had her hands full protecting some dwarven children from a band of six vicious bardes. The warrior woman was not the king's top soldier for nothing. She fought with the courageousness of a pyren and the flair of a dragon. Levantia swung her short sword back and forth both countering attacks and delivering fatal thrusts. After three or four bardes fell lifeless to the ground, the other two bardes fled to gather reinforcements.

"This is not the place for the battle," Glantis thought watching the bardes reassemble. Glantis called out the order to flee. Any further loss of life would hinder their plans to fight another day with the force of the entire dwarven army.

"Retreat!" Glantis yelled. The offensive was broken off, and the whole brigade ran toward the outer edges of town as planned. Glantis caught Grey and told him to try to lead them around the lake to Kratz. The tired dwarf acknowledged the order. Staring at Glantis for a moment, Grey considered the possibility of never seeing him again.

"I know. Now go on. May the gods be with us," Glantis answered, reading the dwarf's hesitant thoughts. Grey quickly ran off leading the dwarves out of the town. Glantis met up with his friends who were now guarding the rear of the group. As soon as he saw they were all right, he smiled. He explained to his friends where Grey was going, and they followed from behind. The four of them ran as fast as they could. Glantis helped Drek along. The mage had once again exhausted himself.

Drek shook Glantis, drawing his attention to a green-robed man exiting his home. The vate waited until the bulk of them passed before walking out into the street. The druid raised his hands to cast a spell.

"Do not let him cast that spell," Drek muttered under his breath. The vate did not see the four companions and, therefore, had his back to them.

Levantia was way ahead of Drek. In the Kantar Mountains, she had seen the hands of a vate rise like that before. She drew her dagger and threw it hard toward the unknowing vate. The dagger flew through the air and struck its target with accuracy. The sharp weapon hit the vate just in time to disrupt his spell. The green-robed vate's hands struggled to reach the dagger in his back. Within moments, he fell backward driving the dagger deeper into his body.

"Go in that house. He is probably the keeper of the town. He may have vital information," Drek said with a heavy breath. The companions rummaged through the home. Someone knocked down a lantern by mistake, and soon the house was bright with fire. Seeing maps of some sort on the druid's table, Drek grabbed them, placing them within his robes.

"Everyone out!" Glantis screamed. The others fled out the door. Seconds later, Glantis came crashing out of the fire-stricken house carrying a bundle of brown and green robes.

"What are those for?" Levantia asked in bewilderment.

"Disguises," Glantis answered, "never know when we might need them." Having lost his own pack, Glantis stuffed the robes into Surlonthes' backpack.

Grey Thornstar had led the dwarves out of the city and had managed to reach Blackwater. Bardes were everywhere.

It took a long time to move because groups of bardes kept ambushing them. When the dwarves reached the edges of Blackwater, they halted for a moment. Grey looked to the south of the lake and viewed a rather large band of bardes heading toward them. Seeing no other way, Grey led the group around the lake to the north. The dwarves rapidly ran around the outer edges of Blackwater. So as not to lose any time, they followed the edges as closely as possible. By this time, the bardes had reached the spot they had stopped at.

Grey and the dwarves were running almost twice as fast as the bardes. The older dwarves, however, were beginning to slow. Even the younger dwarves began to experience difficulty. Forced to work the mines with little food and sleep, it was no wonder why all the dwarves began to fatigue. The pace lagged a bit, but they still maintained a good lead. They were strong and wanted freedom. They would even challenge fatigue in a fight to the death.

Out of nowhere, a horde of bardes appeared from the woodland in front of them. Before Grey could react, the clever bardes had formed a hook around them. There was no escape. Seeing no practical way out, Grey swore in disgust. In the old dwarf's eyes, the lake was definitely not an option. He would rather fight his way out. The sudden touch of another dwarf startled Grey. It was a young male, taller than Grey but much thinner. The boy was pointing.

"Sir, if we can maybe reach those old boats, we might be able to cross the lake."

Grey shuddered at the thought but knew there was no other choice. He clapped the young dwarf on the back saying, "Good eye, son." They would perish if they stayed to fight. At least on the lake, they had a chance. How much of a chance Grey did not know. Maybe the forst was dead.

The bardes were now only a few yards away. Grey and the band, surrounded, had no choice but to run down to the lakeshore. They scurried down the muddy cliff. At the base of the cliff, just in front of the water itself, the mud was at its deepest. Grey tramped through the mud lifting his legs as high as they would go to prevent from sinking. Grey struggled to get to the boats. As much as he hated the wretched idea of attempting to cross Blackwater, he felt he should be one of the first to enter the murky waters.

The bardes, seeing the dwarf's intentions, tried to change directions in order to block them off from the boats, but the dwarves reached the boats in time.

Grey began to untie the old boats from the nearby trees and bushes. As the dwarves arrived, Grey filed them into the boats, filling each craft to its maximum capacity. As the last dwarves were filling the boats, Grey and his crew had already cast off. The boat drifted across the lake. Blackwater extended almost a half mile in every direction.

"Our best bet is to head toward the town of Kratz. There we can get off and run the rest of the way to King's Cove," Grey spoke. Seeing the scared faces of his dwarven friends, he spoke out again. "Worry not, my friends. I have arranged for the dwarves from Dry Rock to meet us with boats on King's Cove. They will then take us to Lore for hot food and water." Smiles appeared on the tired faces of the men, women, and children. The sound of hot food and baths warmed their hearts.

Before the angry bardes reached the lake's edge, every single dwarf was in a boat and out on the lake. The frenzied group of bardes was throwing daggers, stones, and anything else they could find on the muddy bank.

Seeing the bardes as no longer an immediate threat, Grey turned his attention to the lake itself. The waters were indeed black. A pungent odor emitted from the stagnant water. It was impossible to see very far across the lake because it was still a few minutes before dawn. Traces of sunlight far off on the horizon glowed yet remained dim, covered by the towering trees of the Ancient Woods.

Grey and the others paddled the boats with cold, wrinkled hands. The boats moved through the still water. Grey moved his head from side to side, squinting and looking into the still waters. For a minute, he thought he saw bubbles ascending from the lake's bottom. Others soon began to notice the strange bubbles.

The bardes held position on Blackwater's edge. The druid workers seemed to be laughing. This conduct caused Grey's throat to constrict. He became worried as the bubbles increased. Some of the dwarves panicked and began to stand up in the boat.

"Stay down!" Grey ordered in an unsuspecting roar as a brown vine shot from the water and wrapped half-way around the boat. With no hesitation, Grey grabbed another dwarf's sword and slashed the vine in two. Soon after, other vines followed. One after another, they shot around the boats. The dwarves panicked. Children screamed while men and women struggled to cut the vines loose from the boat. The dwarves looked to Grey for help.

Knowing the creature to be a forst, Grey dismissed the idea of telling them. Tears began to fill Grey's eyes. He had done it again, and now his face conveyed a sense of hopelessness. He had led his people into the death-gripping hands of the forst. He was losing his family all over again.

"Why? Why? I should have let the bardes capture us," the troubled dwarf thought. Seeing the peoples' faces as one of the boats almost tipped over was painful. Grey gave out the orders. He instructed every boat's crew to stay low and cut every vine. Grey became irritated seeing the pleased bardes on the lakeshore.

The dwarves managed to keep the boats afloat for a few minutes. To the dwarves, those few, precious minutes seemed like hours. As they began to tire, the vines began winning the fight. Grey and the other dwarves just about gave up as the vines grasped the boats.

Glantis, Drek, Levantia, and Surlonthes stopped at the top of the hill overlooking Blackwater.

"Does anyone see a sign of Grey?" Glantis asked breathing hard.

"Look! Out there," Levantia pointed, her face turning pale. "They're on the lake!" she screamed.

Glantis and the others adjusted their heads toward the lake.

"They must have been forced out onto the lake in order to escape," Levantia surmised. "Grey must have been forced out there by the bardes."

Glantis focused on the bardes. They were laughing and throwing things at the dwarves. The giant warrior's hands clenched. His teeth ground together. He was sickened by these druid followers.

"Glantis, one of the boats just tipped over!" Surlonthes reached for Glantis. Only when the prince reached over, Glantis was gone.

Grey Thornstar's boat was the last afloat. All the other dwarves were treading water. It seemed the forst was playing with them, waiting until the last boat capsized before it pulled them under and digested them all.

Grey and his crew struggled to stay afloat. In moments, the vines overwhelmed the last rowboat. Grey and his entire crew jumped clear of the boat at the last second. Now everyone treaded water above the bloodthirsty forst. Women screamed in the night air as the forst pulled their children under the black waters.

Just as all hope seemed lost, the dwarves began to point to a far bank. Grey turned in the water looking to the lakeshore. From the highest hill above the lake, shot a shimmering blue light across the night's sky, like a shooting star. The shimmering light hit the water and sank below. The further it sank into the forbidden depths the more the light diminished.

Glantis Trefmore sprinted toward the lake. As soon as he came to the incline leading down to the water, he jumped. It was a leap of faith. The warrior's body shimmered blue as he flew through the air. The power surged throughout his body.

The dwarves began to give up. Only Grey, the two boys, and their father remained hopeful. They still believed it to be that heroic man, that healer, who called himself Glantis Trefmore.

The lake remained dark. The one thing that did stop, however, was the vines pulling down any more dwarves. Grey looked all around for any change in the lake's surface.

Grey began to speak out to Glantis, "You may save us now, brave warrior, but I am afraid the damage has been done. All the children have already been taken from their parents," the sad dwarf said, thinking about his family.

The whole lake flashed blue. Again and again it flashed. On the fifth or sixth flash, the light remained constant. Grey and the dwarves watched as the glorious blue light slowly ascended to the surface. The light spread across the entire lake. To everyone's surprise, a man came shooting out of the water, crashing through the lake's glassy surface; the water no longer muddy and black, but clear and glowing blue. The gleaming water ran down the warrior's face and down his axe. Glantis stood with his axe in hand glowing with a blinding light. It was indeed an essence of good given to him. Even the dwarves who did not know of him as Grey did, knew he was not a normal human being. The huge warrior was standing on the water.

Then the light began to lift every dwarf in the water. Grey felt a hard surface strike his feet beneath him. Before he knew it, he was standing on top of the water, his feet held up by the strange blue light, which acted as a sheet of ice. Grey looked around in astonishment as he saw all his crew also rise up next to him. Soon, every dwarf stood upon the strange light. Mothers and fathers screamed in joy as they saw their children standing next to them. It seemed impossible to them how the children could have held their breath so long. Grey heard this question asked and heard an astonishing reply from one of the children. It seems while they were struggling for air, the blue light hit the water, and then they could breathe.

Drek, Levantia, and Surlonthes sprinted out onto the lake, running toward Glantis. Glantis looked at them with glowing blue eyes. They pointed behind him.

Bardes, one, then two, then hundreds piled onto the lake. Grey saw this also and yelled out commands to run.

Another strange thing occurred to Grey as he led the group toward the lakeshore. Just minutes ago, these dwarves were haggard and undernourished. Now, it seemed they had the strength to run around the world. Dismissing this phenomenon, Grey ran up to one of the older dwarves. "How many dwarves remain imprisoned at Kratz?"

"None," the middle-aged dwarf said with a smile. "They just recently transferred all of us to Partha for security reasons."

The new destination was King's Cove and then safely to Lore, but they were not out yet. A more pressing matter was at hand. The bardes, attempting to attack, forced the dwarves to make their final escape.

As the dwarves ran from the bardes, Glantis and Grey met up with their companions. Grey relayed to everyone about the prisoners all being moved to Partha. The others smiled, relieved by the news.

Glantis, however, showed no emotion. The big warrior ran onto the shore of Blackwater. He watched as the last dwarf stepped onto the shoreline. At that very moment, Glantis' eyes flared blue and then went dark. His body faded of light. The only light that shined was that of the new morning sun.

The lake flashed and turned gray in the sunlight. Every barde standing upon the lake sank into the gray waters. The helpless bardes splashed and kicked in horror. Little did they know that the forst was at the bottom of the lake, disintegrated into a murky ash.

Glantis balanced himself against a tree. His companions laughed at the panicking bardes swimming and splashing each other. They slapped each other on the back and walked up the shore's hill to the forest beyond. Glantis stayed to watch the dwarves escape into the forest, heading toward King's Cove. They would be safe now because the dwarves knew this territory well. They had done it. The dwarves were free. Somehow, he knew they would make it to Lore. The now full-morning sun promised sweet freedom for all dwarven-kind alike.

CHAPTER 9
THE MOONPOOL

THE SUN REACHED ITS hottest point. The thick trees of the Ancient Woods blocked the majority of the bright rays. The high temperatures affected the companions. Since they had broken off from the dwarves, the heat had increased. Their rate of travel was slowing so much that they had to stop and rest for a short period. Food was scarce on this arid day. Many of the animals were in their dens avoiding the heat. If they were to find any animals, it would be near a cool stream, and the only water they knew of was Blackwater Lake some twenty miles behind them. Lucky for them, they carried packs filled with food, although they still had no water and would need it soon.

Drek reached into his robes pulling out the maps he had taken from the vate's house in Partha. He studied them for long moments of silence. Then Drek spoke, his voice the first to break through the dry air.

"Gullon was correct in his assumptions."

They all looked at Drek to elaborate.

"I'm certain the druids are shipping the supplies out to sea from Quin." The mage turned the map to face the companions pointing at the tower of Quin. "This is Quin. It's the second tower we know of. If you look at these lines, you'll see that the supply ships are heading out to sea toward the southeast to somewhere they call Fos." Drek ran his fingers along the already drawn shipping routes until he reached the point labeled Fos.

"We have to get on one of those ships," Glantis acknowledged.

"Yes," Drek rubbed his bony fingers along his chin, "these shipping courses run close to Castle Brendonia." Drek set the maps on the ground pointing to the castle's relative location.

"Why do the lines curve?" asked Glantis.

"Yes, it's as if they're trying to hide or go around something," Drek whispered almost to himself, "something big."

The companions traveled long and hard the rest of the day. As nightfall cast its shadows through the forest's trees, the sounds of splashing water floated into their eardrums. Glantis and his friends were sitting crouched behind some rocks along the shoreline. Giant boulders of hard stone covered the shoreline. These heavy rocks were definite proof that the continent had partially divided. While many rocks and boulders sank into the New Sea, others rested upon the shoreline as a sign of the aftermath.

The waves of the New Sea washed up between the rocks raising the water level to their ankles. Surlonthes slowly made his way over to Glantis.

"Where is he?" Surlonthes asked Glantis. The two warriors raised their heads above the rocks looking along the shoreline. The moon reflected sparkles of light off the bubbling water splashing upon the seashore. They waited for the return of Drek. The mage seemed to have regained his strength since they left the town of Partha. Drek insisted on scouting out the supply ships docked at Quin by himself. Meanwhile, the four companions watched for any signs of the mage.

Levantia kneeled next to Grey holding her sword in her right hand. Grey mumbled something about Drek being unpredictable.

Glantis brought his head up, once more looking for his foster father.

In an instant, a cloaked shadow appeared next to Glantis. Startled, both Surlonthes and Glantis turned around. Placing his pale hand to his pursed lips, Drek motioned them to be silent. "There is a boat just beyond those rocks." Drek pointed down along the seashore. "It's loaded with an abundance of supplies, most of which are food, water, and weapons." Drek smiled, seeing the two giant warriors grin at the mention of things to eat. The hard day's journey had cost them all of their food.

Grey and Levantia huddled behind Drek. "Did someone say food?" Grey asked with a sincere look. They all laughed, remembering the old dwarf's ability to eat more than even Glantis.

Drek explained about the ship and hurried them on along the shoreline. The boat was ready to leave port. The companions followed Drek on a concealed path along the shore. Within moments, they arrived at a grouping of rocks. They all climbed over and around them. Several boats were anchored near the shore on the other side. Only one of the boats had its sails raised and was ready to untie from the wooden docks.

"We must hurry," Drek whispered.

"Wait," Glantis commanded. The giant boy grabbed Surlonthes' backpack. Glantis pulled out the bundle of brown and green robes he had grabbed from the vate's home in Partha. Seeing the barde and vate robes, everyone caught on to what Glantis had in mind.

A small barde watched from his post as the ships began to untie from the docks. The barde carried a short sword and several daggers in his belt. He watched as the last supplies were loaded onto the ships. The barde looked up seeing five robed figures walk along the docks toward one of the ships. The barde stood upright seeing that two of them were vates led by three smaller bardes. The barde snickered, noticing one of the barde's shortness. The five druids passed him saying nothing. The barde let out a deep breath. He did not have to worry. The vates had not taken any notice of him. Relieved, the barde leaned back against one of the dock posts and watched the first ship sail across the New Sea. The barde had no idea that he let Glantis and his companions sneak onto the druid ship.

"Commander Vincent. Troops from the castle are crossing the Jade River!" a messenger yelled above the sounds of his horse's clicking hooves. The messenger dismounted his horse and addressed his commander in the first hours of morning.

Vincent was second in command of the Brendonian army. Since Janestin remained stationed with the elves in Torka, the king sent Vincent to handle the gnome dispute.

Vincent stood an average height but always looked taller because of his thin frame. His jet-black hair matched his distinguished-looking mustache hanging from his upper lip.

The messenger approached him.

Vincent said, "Round up the men and tell them the King of Brendonia has been true to his word. The promised troops have arrived."

The messenger turned around. After remounting his horse, the messenger rode back into camp.

Vincent waited on the edges of camp for the new troops. After several minutes, he heard the distant sounds of hooves kicking up earth. Louder and louder, the thundering beats reached his ears. The commander smiled as the troops sent by King Hestin came into sight. He was pleased. The troops were some of the finest in the army. The king was taking a serious gamble sending such a large group of his choice soldiers.

The first officer recognized his commander and slowed the some 500 soldiers.

"Greetings, commander," the first officer said. He saluted by placing his right hand across his chest forming a fist. "The king has placed us at your service." The rest of the soldiers saluted by hitting their metal gauntlets against their breastplates.

Vincent then spoke out to all of them. "Gather at the opposite edge of camp with the others and ready for battle." The horses passed into the camp leaving Vincent behind. The tired-looking commander lowered his head. This was not the first time he had led troops into battle. War was crude and fought for foolish reasons. Vincent let out a deep breath. If only the gnomes would share the water from the Moonpool. The commander walked into camp toward his brave troops. On this quiet morning, he would lead over 1,000 men into another gruesome battle, a slaughter, really. The gnomes did not stand a chance.

Sounds of armor clanged as the riders directed their horses into line. The troop leaders were ordering men into assigned ranks. Then everything changed as one of the troop leaders gave the signal to quiet everyone down. The thousand-plus soldiers responded, and the conversations fell into silence.

Vincent burst out of his tent, half in the process of strapping on his breastplate. A loud, blaring horn echoed through the forest, which seemed to sound from every direction. Two troop leaders and a messenger rushed toward Vincent both shouting, "Gnome war horns, commander!"

Vincent yelled out several commands. "Mount up the forces and wait for my orders!" Vincent turned and went into his tent. An officer stood waiting for him with the rest of his armor. When the soldier finished placing and securing the armor, Vincent ordered him to leave. The officer left the commander's tent carrying his own helmet under his arm as Vincent reached down and scooped up his helm.

"It looks as though they're going to attack us first," Vincent thought. He was disgusted with this whole concept of fighting for water. There was no reason why the gnomes could not share water from the Moonpool. Since the kingdom's reserve water was almost used up, the king had no other choice but to ask the gnomes for help. Maybe that was one of the problems. The gnomes always seemed last on the king's list for everything. Perhaps they were sick of the way the king ignored them. Whatever it was, today's battle was not going to be an answer to the problem.

The battle-ready commander burst out of his tent. His horse stood tied to a nearby tree. The horse was a deep black color and stood many hands high. Vincent quickly untied his horse from the tree, mounted, and took up the reins. Grasping a strong, yet lightweight, long-sword with his left hand and clenching the reins with his right, the commander urged his horse forward. The long-legged stallion responded. This was Vincent's prize horse. He had raised and trained the mount himself. The horse's black color offset Vincent's shimmering armor. They galloped over to the outer edges of the camp where horse-mounted men stood in their assigned areas.

When the commander rode past, the troops became dead silent. Once again, the gnome war horns blasted, echoing throughout the encampment.

"Brendonian soldiers," Vincent addressed. "As you probably know, the king has given us permission to launch a full attack. King Hestin has left all the details for me to decide. I wish you to kill, but only in defense will you kill. Our goal is to hold the area surrounding the Moonpool. Not," Vincent stressed from the bottom of his diaphragm, "not to wipe out the gnome race or even blemish it. The gnomes have refused us water. As you well know, our people in lower Brendonia and the troops stationed in Torka with the elves need water, so let this battle be for reasons of life, not death." The commander bowed his head lowering his sword. Every soldier followed Vincent's lead and bowed a moment in solemn silence. A third time the gnome horn blasted. This was the final warning. The third blast signaled that an attack was underway.

"Here they come. Every soldier follows his troop leader's orders at all times. We are all brothers. So let us guard each other as brothers!"

Soldiers kicked up the earth as they guided their horses though the forest. All too soon, the Brendonian men met the gnomes in a clearing beside the Moonpool. The powder-white faces of the gnomes appeared. Hordes of them ran across the battlefields like white clouds. They were a more primitive people. They did not use horses because of the difficulty they had riding them. The majority of the gnome people were short with bulky, overdeveloped muscles. The gnomes had the will to fight for whatever reasons they believed. Their faces wrinkled with the rage of war. Both male and female fought in all battles. There was no gender discrimination. They worked and lived in equality. The role of the male and female was the same.

The two armies met in a clash of steel. The gnomes struggled to hit the Brendonian warriors who sat high upon horseback. The gnomes adapted their techniques and began to swing swords at the horse's legs. This brought the men down to their level. The fighting lasted for hours. For a time, Vincent's army surrounded the gnomes like cattle and herded them away from the Moonpool attempting to wear them out. Things went well for a short time and casualties were low. Then something happened. As the gnomes scurried into the forest, they somehow doubled back and began to attack from behind. As if that was not enough, hundreds of concealed gnomes swung out of trees ambushing the Brendonian men. They were surrounded.

The gruesome reports came to Vincent from sick-looking messengers. They were actually losing. "Send for more men. They're walking all over us," Vincent dictated the sentence to the messenger stressing that he tell the king those exact words. With great promptness, the messenger took off with great speed, riding on one of the fastest horses in the king's stables.

A tear came to Vincent's eye. The thought of this useless fight threatened to rip his heart in two. He hated neither side and loved both men and gnome alike. "Forward!" the commander cried kicking his horse and raising his sword as he rode into battle.

CHAPTER 10

FOS

THE NOONDAY SUN HID beneath an overcast sky leaving the day gray and dismal. Levantia sat under a heavy, green canvas holding her knees up to her chest. She had lifted a small portion of the cumbersome tarp to look out on the ocean. The New Sea reflected the gray haze of the clouds. The sea had been very calm since the companions' departure from the tower of Quin. The ship sailed all night propelled by a strong, constant wind.

As Levantia turned her head to look back at her friends, a bright twinkle caught her eye and then disappeared. Levantia scanned the horizon with her tired eyes. Again, she saw the bright sparkle of light flicker. Levantia looked up at the sky noticing that the sun was straining to shine through the clouds. She waited for the clouds to pass over and then returned her gaze to the sea. The sparkle glittered on and off until the sun ducked behind another cloud.

"Grey!" Levantia said. She grabbed his shirt and shook him awake. The groggy dwarf opened his eyes mumbling.

"What is it?" Grey asked, sitting up.

"Look out straight in front of the ship's bow," Levantia pointed.

Grey scooted past her and stuck his head out just under the ship's stern rail. He watched for several moments until he saw the extraordinary, bright twinkle. Startled by the flash, Grey lifted his head smashing it into the stern rail.

"Ouch!" Grey hollered. The dwarf held the back of his head with one hand while closing his eyes. When Levantia tried to comfort him, Grey just grumbled. Levantia could not help but laugh. She turned her head not daring to let the dwarf see her. She left Grey and crawled over to where the others slept.

Drek opened his eyes from his deep meditation. He scanned the crawl spaces between the cargo crates until his eyes focused upon the young woman.

"What is it?" he rasped, angered at the interruption.

"Grey and I caught sight of something, possibly land," Levantia spoke in hushed tones. Levantia looked at the two unmoving warriors. With a swift motion, she playfully nudged her boot squarely into Surlonthes' rib cage. The tall man bumped into Glantis startling both of them awake. Before the two warriors could speak, Levantia motioned them to follow her. On hands and knees, they followed Levantia along crawl spaces and around wooden crates until she stopped.

"Grey," she whispered. The old, wrinkled face of the dwarf appeared from around a cargo crate. "Let Glantis and Surlonthes see it," Levantia told him, motioning him to move.

Grey nodded and slipped his way past them.

"There is only room for two out there. Be sure not to stick your head out from under the canvas tarp. It wouldn't be wise. One of the crew members might spot you," Levantia warned.

Glantis and Surlonthes nodded while passing by Levantia. The two men crawled until they reached the side of the ship where a hazy light beat upon the deck. They both stared along the sea's horizon. Then a large blinding flash burned into their eyes. The two men squinted, trying to bring it into focus. Their minds raced as they tried to solve this puzzle.

"Let me see," Drek rasped, pulling at Surlonthes' foot. To the prince's surprise, Drek pulled him three or four feet back through the crawl space. Startled, Surlonthes let the cloaked mage pass by without protest. Drek poked his hooded head out next to where Glantis was watching. An unpredictable wind blew under the tarp, pushing Drek's hood off. Drek fumbled with the hood pulling it back over his head.

Glantis gasped, still staring at the New Sea. He had only seen him with his peripheral vision, yet it was enough. Drek's hair was dark and very matted. Its texture looked extremely rough, and in areas were several bald spots wrinkled and multicolored. It looked painful as if it were a fresh burn from an accident with fire. Glantis changed his expression and turned to face Drek.

"It's out there to the right of the bow," Glantis pointed, moving aside so Drek could look. The mage crawled forward turning his head to look.

Glantis stared at the back of Drek's hooded head. "What happened to him?" Glantis asked himself.

Glantis attempted to speak, but Drek cut him off. "Look straight ahead." Drek pointed a crooked finger just right of the ship's bow. Glantis stared and squinted at the water. "I can't see anything."

"Look at the water. Then look to the horizon line."

Again, Glantis scanned the water. Nothing was there, yet something did not seem right. Then the warrior's eyes widened in astonishment. "It's huge. What is it?"

"I think it's some sort of illusion that reflects the water itself," Drek answered.

"But why? What for?" Glantis stumbled upon his words, still staring at the giant structure.

"Camouflage, the druids are hiding something. Notice as we get closer, it becomes more wavy looking. The reflection is breaking up in some areas."

"Why put something out here in the middle of nowhere?" Glantis asked both himself and Drek.

Drek smiled and gestured further south. Glantis turned to look straight off the starboard side, and there it was. The answer to all their questions was sitting just a few miles away. To the south stood the impenetrable towers of Castle Brendonia, its colored flags waving in the noonday breeze.

Glantis' blood thickened and his muscles tensed until he stopped breathing. He relaxed himself and began to focus on a plan. The idea that the druids were only a few miles away from the castle scared him. They could have attacked at any moment.

"Go explain to the others. Tell them to pack up. We're getting off this ship," Glantis ordered Drek in a deep and serious tone. The mage was inclined to protest but somehow knew it was not his place to do so anymore. The possibility of Glantis and him actually having a father-son relationship was foolish. Glantis existed for one reason only. He was created to stop the evil druid, Bernac. The powerful god who had entered that tavern more than twenty years ago was not just coincidence. Power and wisdom had glowed in that man's eyes, and he had disappeared as fast as he had come.

"We all owe my father great thanks. I must not fail him, Drek," Glantis commented to Drek reading his thoughts. Drek's eyes widened. The yellowish bags under his eyes stretched, creating a shiny surface. Glantis said nothing more. Drek, too astonished to speak, made his way back to the others.

Glantis' stare focused toward the east. He looked eastward as if something were calling to him. For an instant, everything that plagued his thoughts disappeared. The druids fizzled out of his consciousness. To the east was a place unfamiliar to all of Brendonia's races. Somehow, Glantis felt this alienation would be a thing of the past in a few years. He sensed something there, something far across the Dragon Skin Mountains. This glimpse into the future faded.

Several minutes passed by until the others appeared behind Glantis. Each companion was packed and ready to go. Glantis turned around seeing them all ready. Each of them wore the dark green robes Glantis had salvaged from the vate's home in Partha before it burned to the ground. Levantia and Surlonthes kneeled next to each other, and Grey kneeled in front of them. The brown robes on Grey covered him. Drek was waiting behind. His eyes were glowing orange.

Glantis remained silent and tilted his head toward the stern rail. He watched for a brief moment before he turned his attention to his friends again. The group watched the strange warrior. He had gone through a complete change since they had all first met. His powers seemed to be limitless now. His demeanor had changed from a humorous boy to that of a serious man. It seemed natural that his companions all looked to him for leadership. Fear of the unknown caused all of them to remain silent, yet they all felt comfortable in his presence.

Their silence and deep thoughts ceased when Glantis cast his dark blue eyes upon them.

"We need to find some ropes, one for each of us," Glantis whispered. "We have to get to the rear of the ship." He began to move past his friends.

"I saw some ropes in a crate near where we slept," Grey told Glantis coming up to his right side. The warrior glanced at Grey and nodded.

Grey wasted no time saying, "Follow me."

The companions crawled around several aisles of crates until they caught sight of Grey again. The dwarf was pulling out ropes from a dry-looking crate. Grey handed each of them a coil of rope.

"This is the plan," Glantis caught all of their attention. "We will make our way to the rear of the ship, tie on, and lower ourselves into the water. We can hold the ropes until we reach whatever that thing is. Once we're close enough, we'll let go of the ropes and swim away from the boat. Any ideas or objections?"

His friends nodded in agreement. Glantis removed his axe from its usual place on his broad back. Surlonthes and Levantia followed by unsheathing their swords. Grey leaned ready on his battered mace. They stared at each other and then looked at Glantis who gave them a forced smile of encouragement and began to move along the crates. He knew his friends were watching him. Glantis felt their gaze and hated it. Since he first experienced the strange power, it began to change his world and the way others looked at him. It seemed everyone was expecting him to have the answers. What if he was wrong? These thoughts flowed through Glantis at high speeds, each bringing up considerable controversy. Glantis was feeling the burden of responsibility.

The special Brendonian taskforce made its way to the rear of the ship. They moved as one, making sure not to tip or bump anything that would reveal their presence. Glantis led them along the starboard side of the ship. They now squatted around fifteen feet from the stern rail. The tarp still covering their movements, the companions continued to approach the rear of the ship.

They moved until Glantis lurched back. One of the few druids on the ship was standing close to their position. He was dressed as a barde but looked like he belonged to a much higher class. This troubled Glantis. All the bardes he had seen at Esu and Partha were small and lightly armed. This particular barde was a bit taller. The cloak he wore had trouble hiding his thick frame. He held a colored sword that looked sharp. The metal was a pale gray and solid looking. It cast no shine like typical metal weapons.

Glantis turned back to the others. They had caught a glimpse of the peculiar barde, too.

"I don't think we should misjudge his abilities, Glantis," Grey whispered, staring at the powerful barde. Glantis turned his head toward Drek. The mage shook his head having never seen the like of this druid.

"He seems to be moving around. His position is unpredictable. Let's see if we can't slip by him. Leave everything, even what food we can spare. Everyone take off your druid cloaks and put them in your pack. Bring only your ropes and weapons." Glantis waited until everyone removed his pack and cloak. Levantia took all the items and hid them down an aisle where the druids would not so readily find them, at least not until they were long gone.

Glantis took another look. Seeing no sign of the barde, he turned to his friends. "If he spots you, keep going. I'll take him from behind." Surlonthes began to protest but Glantis interceded. "It's the only way." The prince fell silent, gripping his sword. Glantis ignored the stubborn warrior and pulled Grey to the front. "Walk quickly and do it as silently as possible. When you make it to the rear, crawl over and tie your rope to the boat and hold on." Grey stepped forward. Glantis' huge hand grasped his shoulder pulling him back, "Once you walk out from under the canvas, you're in plain sight." Glantis now stared into the dwarf's eyes. "Be careful, friend."

Grey gave Glantis a half-smile. "Someone as old as I am ought to know quite a bit about being careful." Grey let out a short cackle, checked if the way was clear and took off. In moments, the companions watched Grey's little feet go over the ship's stern rail.

Levantia was next. She sheathed her sword and gripped the rope with two hands. Within seconds, she, too, went over the side. Then went Drek, who seemed to be the quietest thus far. The mage's black robes fluttered in the wind as he seemed to float over the side. Still no sign of the barde's reappearance, the prince took off toward the aft of the ship.

Suddenly, with a booming crash, the barde's feet landed on the aft deck just paces in front of Glantis. With his back toward Glantis, he unsheathed his pale gray, bladed sword with the intent of killing Surlonthes. The prince kept running. Before the muscular barde could even begin to chase him, Glantis was on him.

Binding hands landed upon the barde. With no feeling of resistance, Trefmore smashed his head into a heavy, wooden crate, rendering the guard unconscious on the deck of the ship. Glantis dragged him under the canvas. Grabbing his rope and placing the barde's gray sword between his teeth, Glantis ran to the ship's rear, tied on, and climbed over the side. He lowered himself into the water. The ship pulled the companions through the water. So far, they remained undiscovered.

The water was cold, and it chilled their bodies upon contact. The brisk temperature of the water caused Glantis to bite upon the barde's sword blade.

The boat began to turn, revealing an open view of Castle Brendonia. It was about an hour or so past noon. Clouds still covered the sky, blocking out the brilliant sun.

Then the boat started to turn, swinging the companions to one side, and then they saw it. The ship entered an enormous structure. Two mirror-like images opened like doors, creating an entrance large enough for the entire sailing ship to enter. As the ship was almost inside, Glantis saw a formation of land between the mirror-like structures and the cavern the ship was entering. He motioned everyone to let go of the ropes and swim to the gap.

Surlonthes noticed men on planks beside the ship. Just inside the camouflaged gates, bardes were helping to dock the ship. Seeing it as a risk, Surlonthes yelled out, "Duck under!"

The companions took no time to look around. They released the ropes and went underwater.

One by one, they resurfaced. Glantis came up last, seeing the almost invisible doors close. If he had not known where they were, he would have never seen the doors even from this close range. The freezing companions swam to the gap. Grey reached it first, climbing up behind the mirror-like camouflage. The camouflage blocked off the wind. Grey smiled, telling them, "It's much warmer behind this stuff." As another blast of cold air flowed over the others, they raced to reach the gap.

The doors began to open again, giving them even more reason to hurry. Glantis was the last one because of all the extra weight he carried. He backed far into the hole making sure he remained out of view. The giant doors came to a lurching stop, now fully open. Out came a different ship heading back toward the tower of Quin.

"This is a regular shipping lane," Surlonthes stated. "Look, there are more of those powerful bardes."

"Yes, they're planning a major attack on the castle," Drek explained.

"What? How do they expect to take over the castle with the thousands of troops guarding its walls," Surlonthes argued, raising his voice.

"Think, prince!" Drek rasped.

"Yeah, think, prince," Grey helped.

Surlonthes gave a look of cold anger to the dwarf. Grey stared back innocently.

Drek, ignoring the immature conflict, continued, "The king has been sending troops to help the elves, and who knows where else since we left the castle. At the time of our departure, a good sum of the Brendonian army was sent to Torka," Drek finished, directing his attention to the camouflage. "These mirror-like shields cover this whole island, hiding it from the king and everyone in lower Brendonia," Drek explained, running his hand along one of them.

"Are they breakable?" asked Glantis, walking up to touch them.

"Stand back," Surlonthes said, grabbing hold of Grey's mace and pulling it from the dwarf's hands.

The prince lifted the heavy weapon, "How do you carry this, dwarf? It weighs more than you," he grunted.

Grey began to protest, but Surlonthes had already taken a swing. The end of the mace smashed against the shield. It had done something, but from the sound of the hit, the shield was beyond solid. Unsatisfied with the first blow, Surlonthes took another swing. This time the mace hit with a hollowing note, bouncing off with greater force. It seemed the mace was only scratching the surface of a single layer. Surlonthes choked up for a final swing, but Glantis protested.

"Forget it. Even if we could break it after five hits or so, it would take three days to break enough for the king to see the island." Surlonthes listened to his reason and reluctantly handed the mace back to Grey.

"What we need is something more forceful," Drek told Glantis.

Glantis began to fear the answer and suggested looking around the island. He knew one of them would ask him to use his power. He was not even sure if he could use it. If only the shields were flammable, then Drek could burn the camouflage shields all in a matter of minutes.

They climbed up rocks moving away from the reflecting shields. Steel beams supported the shields, which were stacked up on edge until both the perimeter and the height of the island were invisible. The island was the only thing that did not sink low enough for the New Sea to cover. Something had held it up after the division of the continent. The companions had no doubt that Bernac had created this with his magical powers. While they were climbing rocks, Drek mentioned that the mirror-shields were probably in place even before the druid highmaster sank the land.

Preoccupied with the hard climb, the companions failed to notice that Grey had disappeared.

"Grey, this is no time to wander off," Glantis began to call him in a low, penetrating voice. The prince began to mumble.

Glantis held up his hand for silence. The sound of tumbling rocks grew louder. The party unsheathed their weapons.

Grey came hobbling up the mountainside breathing hard and saying at the same time, "…Ships…hundreds."

"Catch your breath, friend," the prince helped him up to a flatter surface. "Slow down and tell us."

The wheezing dwarf caught his breath. "They have hundreds of ships and thousands of men, good men, not the smaller bardes with which we've dealt. They're more like the ones on the ship," the dwarf paused as traces of shame crossed his face. "They saw me and are coming this way. I'm sorry." He looked down, "I failed all of you!"

There was no time to admonish the dwarf. Everyone turned to Glantis, who was staring down the rocky hillside. He seemed to be watching the little pebbles roll down the hill from where Grey had come. "More like you've saved Castle Brendonia," Glantis said, still eyeing the hill. The rocks began to pick up speed and then harmlessly hit the shields. Glantis snapped out of his trance saying, "How long before they'll reach us?"

"A good five minutes, it's possible they have other escape areas leading up here, but not enough to make much difference. I went back down toward the doors and found only one entrance leading into the shipping docks."

"I have an idea, but we still need a way off this island," Glantis clenched his fists.

"Leave that to me." Drek placed his hand upon Glantis, revealing a crooked smile.

King Hestin stood upon his battle tower discussing the letters sent to him by his commanders.

"Sire," his advisor persisted, "Vincent needs more support. If we hold off much longer, Vincent and his men will be slaughtered. By then, it won't matter whether our troops reach there or not. The castle has not been threatened since this whole thing started."

"That's what scares me," the king spoke, rubbing his chin.

"My liege, you must make a decision," the advisor concluded.

The king looked out in all four directions searching for signs of his son. That was the reason for his indecision. He was worried about his son. The king was not one to be negative. He somehow knew his son was still alive. His wife had died years ago. Surlonthes, his only child... he could not bear to think about it. These things were clouding his judgment.

The king decided that it was time to act. He would send the majority of the castle's troops to the Moonpool.

A sudden wind blew over the castle tower, almost knocking down the king and his advisor. The enormous span of Plolate's wings rose over the tower walls. The great bird was flying northeast toward the New Sea. The ocherous' speed was astounding. Plolate screeched as he flapped his wings with fierce velocity.

The king regained his balance watching the bird fly away, saying to his advisor, "Keep the troops here another hour."

Glantis Trefmore lowered his hands upon a huge boulder. The giant rock towered over Glantis' six-foot frame. The stone's breadth was enough to hide all of them. Glantis searched his mind for the power given to him by his true father.

Then he felt the blue energy begin to surge throughout his body. It concentrated in his hands. He pressed them against the boulder transferring the energy to it. The rock broke loose from its foundation and plunged down the rocky hillside. As they watched the boulder gather speed, other rocks began to follow.

"Now!" Glantis yelled, his voice echoing across the New Sea.

Drek raised his white, bony hands. Curling his fingers, the dark mage's eyes glowed fiery red. Two concentrated, threadlike strands of red fire burst from Drek's hands. Drek snapped back his wrists lowering his hands to his sides. The companions watched as the stream of fire continued through the air until it collided with the huge boulder. The fire enveloped it and shattered the stone into pieces sending super-heated shards of rock at incredible speeds into the camouflaged shields. The rocks ripped through the shields, shattering them like glass.

Glantis stood at a giant formation of rock. This was not a boulder. It was actually a cliff standing over fifteen feet tall. Glantis placed his hands upon it, and after a few seconds, the rock formation broke loose and plowed down the hillside. Drek followed by shooting four streams of fire at different sections of the stone slab. The fire covered and pulled the rocky mass apart. The flying fragments destroyed the shields, exposing the southeast side of the island. They had done it. It was now visible to Castle Brendonia.

Large numbers of bardes were storming out of escape holes armed with swords. All of them sought revenge upon the companions who stood in the open, outnumbered. The bardes were enraged at the damage done to Fos, the highmaster's secret island. Soon, their faces reflected an expression of utter grief. They knew they were beaten when they saw what screeched in the skies above.

The great ocherous, Plolate, swooped down from the sky landing next to the companions. They mounted the giant bird that then flew them to Castle Brendonia. Plolate screeched in discomfort as a wide-eyed dwarf clenched his hands onto his feathered neck.

"A little higher than you're used to, Grey?" Surlonthes laughed aloud. Though Grey would make up for it later, he did not feel like arguing with the prince.

CHAPTER 11

THE BATTLE FOR BRENDONIA

"WHAT IS IT?" the king bellowed. "I need privacy. I have many decisions to—"

"Sire, please! You know I would never cut you off, but you simply must come up to the tower and see this for yourself," the advisor pleaded, motioning the king to follow.

King Hestin rose from his seat with a sigh and followed. The advisor wore a red tunic and a blue cape flowed from his neck, the Brendonian insignia upon his chest in brilliant black and gold colors.

The king and his messenger commenced to climb the tower stairs. Hestin swore he had climbed these stone stairs one too many times. When they reached the top, the advisor pointed northeast, "Look, Sire, the island."

Hestin's mouth quivered, "In the name of lords, where did it come from?"

"I do not know, my lord. I only know that I saw flashes of fire, and then it appeared, just part of it, then the rest, I only saw it a moment—"

An echoing screech cut the advisor off. Plolate was flying at great speed toward the castle. Only this time, the great bird carried passengers.

"This way, Sire, he is going to land on the tower!" The advisor grasped the king and pulled him down the stairwell as the giant, yellow claws of Plolate perched upon the tower's ledge. The screeching sound of the ocherous' talons digging into the solid stone rang in their ears.

"It's my son!" The king threw the advisor off him. King Hestin ran out to meet Surlonthes who was the first off the giant bird, not including Grey, who either jumped or fell onto the ground in order to throw-up his most recent meal.

The king passed by the gagging dwarf, embracing his son. Hestin then began to hug the others.

"No time," Glantis told the king. "I need a good 300 feet of rope. We also need four horses, now!" Glantis was now ordering the king's advisor. The man, dizzy and confused because the king had thrown him aside, scurried back down the staircase to get the supplies.

Glantis explained about the druids' plan to empty the castle and attack from Fos, the island that was now visible. He told the king about Parlock and about Grey Thornstar, who should be honored for saving their lives.

Minutes later, an officer returned with the rope. It was a huge coil of thick rope, comprised of many pieces knotted together.

"This was all the rope we could find. We had to tie pieces together."

"You have done well," Glantis told him, taking the cumbersome coil of rope.

"One more thing, sir, the four horses are ready at the front gates." The officer left.

"Sire," Glantis turned to the king, "send out all your ships and take control of that island. That is the most important site. It's all the druids have."

"Our troops are low on water. The excess we had all went out with our soldiers. Here at the castle, we're at the bare minimum. The soldiers cannot be expected to fight long," the king interceded with the warrior's orders.

"I will return the water," Glantis answered.

"It would take a miracle to unblock that spring in the Kantar Mountains. That place is crawling with more druids than an ant hill has ants," the king said, looking at Glantis.

Glantis' four companions, all talking at once, communicated to the king that it might be possible. The king, having last seen the boy cutting through the stone wall at the castle, did not think the task feasible. However, the changes were obvious in both Glantis' size and features since he left only a week ago. Both physically and mentally, Glantis had changed.

"We have no more time for this," Glantis' voice rose above all the others with assured authority. "Follow me on horseback along the Jade River until you reach the hole we first entered. Take the horses and climb up the mountains. When you reach the top, you will see a huge opening covered with dry brush and dead weeds. Wait for me there."

Glantis hopped upon Plolate, with his axe and the barde's pale metal sword. Holding the rope in one hand, Plolate's thick feathers with the other, he yelled, "To the Kantar's, great bird, as fast as you can!"

Clifford Janestin addressed Brendonia and Torka's soldiers for the last time.

"This is it, my brave soldiers. This is our last chance to push the bardes. Push them so far back that they can only breathe their own brethren's blood." The soldiers cheered at Janestin's speech. Elves and human men were upon their horses ready for battle. With new soldiers from the castle, the thought of victory was strong. The bardes pushed them out the first time. This time it would be the bardes who get pushed back.

Again, the great ocherous, like a sign from the gods, appeared above them swooping down out of the overcast sky. The soldiers looked up watching the impressive bird. Unseen by most since the Boundary Wars, nonetheless, there it flew across Brendonia's sky.

Grengale turned to Clifford. "Look where it's landing. Can you see the man getting off? If my sight does not fail me, I would say that man was none other than Glantis Trefmore."

"It could be. It could be," Janestin repeated, astonished.

"Maybe there's an entrance from the top of the Kantar's down to the spring. Of course! We can place some archers up there for support," Grengale said.

"We could take out large numbers of bardes in seconds," Janestin interjected, feeling the adrenaline pumping through him.

Raising his fists, Clifford Janestin shouted out the order. "Please your king, and serve your lord! Attack, my brave soldiers. Let's get our water back!"

Grengale immediately led a group of archers to the side and gave them their special orders.

The troops rode hard into enemy territory. Riding with victory in their hearts, they felt they must not let the loss of their friends and brothers be for nothing.

Glantis tied the thick rope around a strong rock formation and then began to lower himself down into the cavern. As he did this, Brendonian and elven troops poured into the cavern from the opposite side.

The bardes began to attack, defending the hole.

Glantis, unseen, lowered himself into the blue, swirling hole of water. Immediately, the white void surrounded him as it did before. Only this time there was no falling, only the faint sight of falling water. The water was contained within the hole's amorphous walls by Bernac's magic. The vision cleared, and the once remembered sight of the tower of Esu appeared. He was inside again. Only this time he hung above the water ramp. The rope was too short, and the water was causing Glantis to lose his grip on the rope. Trefmore unsheathed the new sword he obtained from the barde and attempted to swing at the magical crystals that made the hole.

Hit by an invisible energy, Glantis fell off the rope. The warrior fell fast to the wooden floor, slamming against it and shaking the entire tower.

"You shall not escape me again, Trefmore. You've ruined my plans once too often. It won't happen again."

Glantis opened his eyes tilting his head up. Bernac stood at his head, dressed in the blackest of robes towering over him. Glantis stood up attempting to attack with his sword. Bernac's hand grasped Glantis' throat. The highmaster's fingernails were draining the life from the warrior. Glantis dropped his sword and froze. As his weapon clanged on the floor, his eyes closed. Glantis was falling into unconsciousness. He felt the coldness he had suffered at the Darkpath. Visions of Bernac striking him to the ground reentered his mind. The evil druid was draining his life.

Then a picture came to Glantis' mind, a picture of the druid highmaster and a group of green-cloaked vates casting a spell that sank the middle of the Brendonian continent.

It was Bernac. He knew it had to have been, yet now he knew for sure. At this new revelation, Glantis began to fight the coldness. His heartbeat started to increase. His body began to warm. The power flowed through him stronger than ever before.

Bernac, feeling the change, strengthened his grip, crushing and cracking Glantis' neck. Any mere human would have died at this point, but Glantis was not a man.

Glantis' neck began to reform, forcing the master druid's hand to lurch off in pain.

"You have killed and destroyed enough of this world, druid. And now you must pay the final price."

"Wait!" Bernac pleaded. Bernac stared into Glantis' eyes. Reading his mind with a spell, the druid began to speak in a soft voice. "We are not all that different, Glantis. I, too, know how it feels to be abandoned by my parents. Let us not destroy one another. Let's stand together so that no one can ever hurt us again. Together, we can rule this land as it should be ruled, together!"

Bernac's words seemed to hold Glantis from action. Glantis was now staring at Bernac.

"Yes, yes, Glantis," Bernac said, seeing he had discovered a weakness in the warrior. "What has this world done for us? We were born into it alone. We both started at a disadvantage. For us, nothing came easy. You know as well as I, in this world we must take what we want. No one has ever been there to give us any support. Join me, brother."

Glantis was in a trance. Bernac's words touched him. What had he been given? Drek took care of him, yet it was in a way that made him feel different from the other kids. Painful memories filled Glantis, and Bernac did not seem as wicked as before. Maybe he was right.

In an instant, the forest master's warning echoed in Glantis' mind. Golis had said, "Bernac has much in common with you. Don't let him turn your human thoughts to his bidding..."

As if walking out of a fog, Glantis regained his god-like clarity. Golis was right. Bernac was tricking him.

"Bernac!" Glantis called out. "It is true we were both abandoned, but that doesn't make it right to take the lives and possessions of others. Your wicked ways are not the solution to dealing with the world. You leave me no choice."

Glantis Trefmore raised his titan-like hands. Blue sparks shot from his fingers spreading over the druid's body. Bernac yelled in horror. As the scattered blue sparks surrounded him, the druid's body began to deteriorate, turning his bone to ash until nothing remained.

Glantis paused, the blue energy calming down inside his inner being. The warrior neither smiled nor frowned. He had acted with hatred and vengeance, and he was not proud of it. Despite what Golis had said about discarding his human emotions, something would not let him. Killing never seemed acceptable to him. He had not the knowledge of a god.

Dousing his thoughts, Glantis sheathed his fallen sword into his belt loop. Changing his mind, Glantis cast the barde's gray-bladed sword aside. He wanted nothing to do with these druid weapons. He stepped up onto the water-catch and leaped up to the rope. The rope connected with his left hand only, and they became one. Nothing would separate his grip. Glantis Trefmore reached to his back, grasping his axe with his right hand. He began to move his body, causing him to swing toward the crystals. The magic had faded since Bernac's death; however, the power of the vates pulsed within it.

Glantis let out a roar. He brought his elven, silver axe down upon the crystal once, then twice. The axe began to shimmer blue. On the third hit, the crystal broke. Glantis then shifted his body on his back swing and broke the other with his great axe. The magic hole began to close. The warrior latched his axe to his back and climbed through the diminishing hole. He found himself holding his breath.

Water filled in around him, and he swam to the surface as the white void vanished under his kicking feet.

Arrows sung a song of peace, striking bardes from the open ceiling of the mountain. Elves and humans fought as one, the bardes beaten. Most of the men were tying ropes to horses, trying to move heavy boulders that blocked the river holes leading out toward the castle. One rock was giving them the most trouble. Men and elves were pushing it and striking it with their swords. This rock had to be removed because it was blocking the main water channel that led to the castle.

To everyone's surprise, red liquid began to spurt from its cracks. Then, all at once, the rock broke open revealing an unborn beast, not yet through its final growing stages. Bloody water poured through the now open hole. Then the water cleared. Clean water was now on its way to the King of Brendonia. Cheers mixed with surprise and elation erupted in the cavern.

An age-old eye opened. Its color was a burning orange. The pupil was darker than night. The dragon queen of the Fire Crypts felt the death of her unborn child.

The fire-red dragon rose from the Fire Crypts to avenge her child.

Syria, queen of the dragons, flapped her aging wings breathing fire as she flew across the continents. In minutes, she reached the New Sea, skimming its waters, cooling her body and throat. With unbelievable speed did Syria shorten the distance between herself and the Kantar Mountains.

"Water!" the lookouts and soldiers along the Jade River yelled. "The Jade River flows with bloodied water, the blood of the bardes. We have won the caverns in the Kantar Mountains," the men yelled. They started gathering the water, sending it on ship to the deserving soldiers on Fos.

The Brendonian troops near Kylar yelled. They, too, were in need of this great savior. The gnomes were fighting like ferocious animals and never seemed to wear out. The fighting stopped and cheering ensued as the Brendonian soldiers witnessed the new freshwater rushing into the Jade River's delta. Commander Vincent called for permanent retreat. The war with the gnomes was over.

Syria was sighted in the air. All fell into an unconscious state. Syria was making a high-screeching sound. The dragon queen was burning up everything she could find. Plolate hesitated at first, waiting for Glantis to return. But seeing the threat of the dragon, the giant ocherous launched off its feet into the air. The ocherous stabbed the dragon with its unbreakable beak. Syria ignored the pain. Knowing her baby was dead, she went into a rage. The dragon queen turned upon Plolate and sent forth a stream of fire. The ocherous flapped its powerful wings and lifted itself with great acceleration, eluding the flames. With great agility, Plolate changed his direction and dived toward the dragon. Syria turned to face the ocherous with bloody eyes. They crashed together with an ultimate force locking up together in the air. With unfathomable strength, the dragon queen hit the ocherous off her with a massive claw sending the mammoth bird flying backward. Plolate struggled hard to turn around, but it was too late. He was vulnerable, and the dragon had him. The dragon queen was an excellent shot. Syria sent forth a fatal stream of fire engulfing Plolate, bringing the trusty bird crashing to the rocks.

Drek and the companions were too late. Drek did not give up, though. He dismounted his horse. The enraged mage struggled forward, his life force drained since the arrival of Syria. Drek crawled forward leaving his friends behind. He was going to avenge Plolate, the wondrous bird and friend.

Drek shot bursts of flames, reaching the dragon, but not harming Syria's scales. The talisman upon Drek's chest burned with a red light. It was draining his innermost power and killing him. Syria turned on the mage, casting out streams of fire formed from her own magical talisman chained around her neck. The dragon queen's talisman resembled Drek's.

As Glantis found safe footing, he pulled himself up the Kantar's ledge, only to see Drek, his foster father, engulfed in flames. Drek's body disappeared. The fire surrounding Drek funneled into the ground. Or was it the ground?

Before Glantis could react, the dragon swooped down picking up Drek's talisman. The dragon queen then flew away to the north and was out of sight in seconds.

Thoughts and visions of both a good and evil nature began to enter Glantis' mind: the dragon protecting her unborn child; Clifford Janestin's army destroying the bardes; Hestin's army winning and securing Fos; visions of Gullon's dwarven army at the Darkpath ridding upper Brendonia of all the druids; laying siege upon the Druid's Keep; bringing its evil stones crumbling to the ground; pictures of Commander Vincent retreating from the gnomes, knowing that the fighting was useless now that Brendonia's water was everyone's to share; and the grandeur of Golis and all of his trees feeding upon the life-giving liquid. Then the visions began to fade.

Without warning, a familiar voice entered Glantis' mind. "East," it called to him. The same voice had spoken to him in the Druid's Keep when he had almost given up. Who was it?

Nevertheless, for the time being it was over. The druids' attempt to take over lower Brendonia had failed, but it left the land scarred. However, the water flowing in the Jade would bring back the wilting land and trees. Time, time is what it would take to heal Brendonia. One thing that might never change was the forever-divided continent. New treaties and boundaries would have to be made between the races as well. The race of druids had been almost wiped out of existence. Even so, the worst of the races' problems were over, or were they? With the destruction of Bernac, perhaps the druids would change their ways. Time would tell.

Glantis had managed to elude his companions. He knew his place was not among them anymore. Several pathways leading into the forest stretched before him. Glantis chose the "greenest path" as Parlock had advised before his death. Perhaps the elf had known Glantis would leave his companions once Bernac and the druids were defeated. Then again, maybe Parlock's words meant something else.

The warrior slipped into the Bimbalian Forest on foot heading east. Only in the east could there be any future for him. He would find answers there. Someone or something there was calling him. Maybe he could live normally in the east. Again, he caught himself with that strange revelation of having a normal life. He knew as well as anyone who knew him. It was just not possible. He had to travel alone from now on. With Drek gone, his deepest ties to Brendonia were cut.

Without warning, Glantis heard a familiar howl. The warrior scanned the forest around him. An animal crashed through some nearby brush both knocking Glantis down and licking his face. It was the pyren, Oonic, bigger than ever. Perhaps he would not travel alone.

ABOUT THE AUTHOR

*G*REGORY *C*HESTER *S*CHOP was born and raised in West Bloomfield, Michigan where he attended West Bloomfield High School. He handwrote the first draft of *Glantis Trefmore – Awakening* during his high school junior and senior years.

He attended college at Michigan State University on a small, academic scholarship that paid for one semester of books. Between 1992 and 2000, he attended three different Michigan-based universities where he managed to earn two degrees in English, as well as a teaching certificate. Much of his tuition was funded by working as a certified fitness trainer.

Greg has worked as a public and private schoolteacher as well as a community college and university professor. He writes in many different genres and aspires to compose a serious piece of literature during his lifetime.

He currently resides in Michigan with his wife and two children.